KISS MOMMY GOODNIGHT

BARBARA NICKOLAE

BERKLEY BOOKS, NEW YORK

KISS MOMMY GOODNIGHT

A Berkley Book / published by arrangement with
the authors

PRINTING HISTORY
Berkley edition / November 1994

ISBN: 0-425-14043-1

BERKLEY®
Berkley Books are published by
The Berkley Publishing Group, 200 Madison Avenue,
New York, New York 10016.
BERKLEY and the "B" design are trademarks of
Berkley Publishing Corporation.

PRINTED IN THE UNITED STATES OF AMERICA

10 9 8 7 6 5 4 3 2 1

For Stacy and Jeff,
a lifetime of happiness

PROLOGUE

Belinda Raymond glanced at the kitchen clock and turned on the electric mixer, then waited impatiently for the frosting in the bowl to take on a glossy, white sheen.

She had managed to get out of the office early, never an easy task. But the cake would be perfect, just the way Lissa liked it, and everything was going to be fine. She would somehow make it up with Ted. It was going to be a wonderful party.

She smiled to herself, picturing Lissa's serious little face as she'd tucked her in the night before.

"Choc'lit cake, Mommy, with fluffy white icing and Winnie the Pooh on top. And Roo, too, and Kanga and Eeyore. And Tigger! Don't forget Tigger!"

Belinda laughed softly and began to spread frosting in smooth little dips and whorls. She was going to have to hurry to finish the cake and get it safely stored away before Lissa got home from her gymnastics class.

She was nearly finished when she heard the back door open. It was much too early for Lissa.

"Belinda?"

She looked up, mildly surprised. "Oh! Yes, I'm in here. But I don't have time to talk. I've got to finish this cake before Judy brings Lissa home."

"That's all right, I understand." He came up and stood behind her. "Pretty cake. Okay if I watch?"

Belinda shrugged. "Of course. It _is_ pretty. Lissa will be pleased. I can't believe she's going to be four!"

She tossed the spatula into the empty bowl and turned the cake to survey it. She was reaching for the package with the little Pooh characters when she felt the first stabbing pain—less a pain, really, than an odd little prickle—as though she'd been pricked by a pin.

She turned around and her eyes widened, but her scream caught in her throat. Then he loomed over her, clamped a hand across her mouth, and brought the knife up high.

She struggled, bracing herself on the table behind her, praying for enough force to topple him, but he pinned her firmly, thighs jammed against hers, and plunged the knife downward—again and again—his face contorted, his breaths great, ragged rasps.

She was falling, falling, sick to her stomach, overcome with dizziness. "Please," she begged, trying desperately to focus through a viscous red haze.

But the face above her flickered and faded, and she felt herself sliding into darkness. . . .

When her eyes fluttered open, she heard herself moan. _Danny. Oh, God. Danny_ . . .

CHAPTER

—1—

Paula Carroll closed her eyes and turned her face up expectantly.

"Gorgeous, gorgeous." Rollie sighed. "A face that could launch a network."

Paula laughed. "Get on with it, Rollie. Forty minutes till airtime."

She felt the familiar dusting of powder, and the feather-light touch of Rollie's fingers roughing up her brows. Next the blusher, mascara, lip gloss—she knew his routine by heart.

"Paula, can you come out here a minute? We need a level on three."

The sound engineer. Paula turned. "Okay, I'll be right there! Hang on, Rollie—stay where you are. I'll just be a minute, I promise."

Holding the makeup cape draped around her, she moved quickly through the room, entered the soundstage, and picked her way carefully through the mass of cables and wires.

It was cool and dim. The studio lights had not yet

been turned on. But the new graphics were already in place behind the horseshoe-shaped, oak desk— *KSFO, The Best of the Bay*, in bold, contemporary script—and even without the hot lights on them, they added grace and elegance to the set.

"Hey, I love it!" Paula smiled, taking her place at the desk. "Al, are you out there?"

"Right here! Thanks," she heard the set designer call. "I keep telling 'em we can make it look just like uptown. All it takes is money!"

"We're live on three, Paula. Gimme a level." The engineer's voice boomed.

Paula wet her lips and smiled at the gesture. Sheer force of habit. "KSFO, the best of the Bay. Good evening, San Francisco. I'm Paula Carroll and—"

"Great. Fine. Recheck one and two."

She swiveled slightly in her seat, facing first camera one, then two, repeating her spiel until the sound men were satisfied.

"That's it, Paula, thanks."

With a last glance at the brilliant blue lettering, she hurried back toward the makeup room. She knew how cranky Rollie could be when he felt he was pushed for time.

"Madame." He gestured broadly toward the chair, and Paula settled into it, as anxious as he was to be done with her face so she could spend a few minutes with her cue cards.

But Rollie took his time, moving around the chair. "I really like the hairdo."

"Thanks. Me, too. You get the credit, and viewer reaction is great."

It was Rollie who'd convinced her to cut her long, tawny mane and go for a newer look—shorter, softer, swept-back curls, sophisticated but feminine—and though her own reflected image still surprised her, she had to admit she liked it.

"Look at those cheekbones." Rollie winked, whisking on some blusher. "And baby blues like Looosiana bayous, sparklin' in the noonday sun."

"Cut it out." Paula fidgeted. "Eyes. Everybody has them."

"Not like those." He tilted her chin and began applying mascara.

"Paula, phone!" A red-haired production assistant leaned into the room.

"Take a message," Paula said, her chin still captive in Rollie's grasp. "I won't take calls this close to airtime. You know that, Betty Lou."

The young woman seemed to hesitate. "You might want to take this one. It's your agent. I recognized his voice. He says it's very important."

Paula sighed. Zachary knew she liked time alone before her broadcasts. "Can you bring me a phone?"

"Got it right here." Betty Lou reached down to plug it in. "There you go. Line two."

Rollie gave her lashes a final fillip and turned to select a lip gloss. She lifted the receiver. "Hello, Zach. You better make this good."

"The best." Zach chuckled. "Just like you. I know, you like your breathing time. So make it count. Be good tonight. Be very, very good."

Rollie showed her a coral lip gloss. She shook her head. "A little lighter. . . . Why, Zach? Get to the point." She nodded at Rollie's next choice.

"Stu Snyder is going to be watching. We just had dinner together. It seems his network could be very interested in Paula Carroll as an anchor."

She held up a finger to let Rollie know she would

only be a minute. "Listen, Zach, so what's new? You've said that about all the networks."

"What's new is Snyder is in the market for sleek, sophisticated, and savvy—a bill you fill on all three counts, and he wants to get a real close look."

Paula made a face. "Savvy, huh? Does that mean he wants a good investigative reporter? Or some airhead mannequin who can simper at the camera and manage not to fluff her lines?"

"To be discussed. That's the next step. First we gotta make him want you. I'll leave you be so you can get it together. I just wanted you to know."

"Thank you, Zach. I have to go." She replaced the receiver and turned to Rollie, who had the good grace to say nothing as he expertly applied her lip gloss.

"Paula, the city council story's been bumped to second lead." Betty Lou reappeared in the doorway. "We'll have live coverage at a murder scene up the coast—I'll leave the new script in your dressing room."

Paula groaned. She'd have little time to study the new lead. She gave Rollie a beseeching look.

"Okay, okay, we're done!" He stepped back to survey his handiwork, but Paula was already on her feet.

"Thanks, Rol." She unfastened the makeup cape and threw it over the back of the chair. "It's perfect. I don't know what I'd do without you."

"Remember me when you move up to network."

She paused, made a face at him, and hurried down the hall to the privacy of her tiny dressing room.

Inside, she glanced at the new script, but there was nothing much she could memorize. All she had to do was cut to Deirdre Adams, who would be waiting live at the crime scene, and Paula thought she could manage that smoothly enough even for Stu Snyder.

She put aside the script and flipped through the cue cards. She wished Zach had not called. He knew as well as she did that she performed well every night, no matter who was watching, and that Channel Eight's share of the news ratings had increased measurably since she'd come back to San Francisco last year.

Besides, it wasn't the first time he'd talked her up to the networks and nothing much had come of it. It *would* happen, she was sure it would happen, but it would happen when the time was right—when she was well enough known that she could write her own ticket and demand some investigative reporting time.

She turned to look at the half-dozen awards that hung on her dressing room wall—proof from news organizations all over California that Paula Carroll had the stuff. At twenty-seven, she'd already accomplished more than a lot of women dreamed of. The rest would happen, too, and when it did, Paula Carroll would be ready.

"Ten minutes, Paula!"

"Thanks, Betty Lou!" But she wasn't ready now. Quickly, she stepped out of a corduroy skirt and into a blue silk suit, picked up her cue cards and the new script and headed out to the set.

Shutting out the noise around her, she sat quietly in her chair and concentrated on staying cool under the barrage of lights. Gradually the pandemonium receded and all eyes focused on her. A deep breath. Wet the lips. Put on the dazzling smile. "KSFO, the best of the Bay. Good evening, San Francisco. I'm

Paula Carroll, and our news tonight takes us live to Seaview, where Deirdre Adams covers a breaking story about a murder only hours old."

"Yes, Paula." The earnest face of the young, black reporter looked at her from the monitor, and Paula looked down to check her lead into the city council story.

"We're here in the eight hundred block of Rutledge Avenue, where late this afternoon a man came home to find his young wife's body sprawled on the kitchen floor. . . ."

Paula had only been half listening, but something she'd heard caught her attention, and she looked at the monitor as the camera panned back to show a view of the house. My God, it was Belinda's house— Belinda and Ted's! She shook her head to clear it.

"The dead woman, identified as Belinda Raymond, had been stabbed several times."

Paula felt sick.

". . . not known at this time how long the woman may have been there before her husband discovered her body. . . ."

She tried to steady herself against the desk, but she felt as though she would crumple.

". . . Fortunately the couple's young daughter, Melissa, was away from home this evening, having dinner at a neighbor's home after returning from a gymnastics class. . . ."

Lissa. Oh, my God. Lissa. . . . Paula couldn't breathe. This couldn't be true. . . . It wasn't happening. . . . But Deirdre's face, back on the monitor, looked more earnest than ever.

"At this hour, police are questioning a man believed . . . calling it a sex crime . . ."

Paula searched the crowd behind Deirdre, looking

for Ted, for Lissa—for Belinda, too, as though the whole story might turn out to be a sick joke. But she recognized no one, and she had to do something— had to get herself together—before the live telecast drew to a close and the show moved back to the studio.

"Paula! Paula! Are you okay?" A cameraman whispered at her side. She stared at him, unable to answer, and the floor man was giving her a sign.

Slowly she felt the color return to her face. She forced herself to take a deep breath. By the time the light came up on camera two, she thought she might be able to speak.

"In local news, it now appears that at least three city council members have reversed their stances and are coming out in favor of a plan to restructure city government. . . ."

Somehow the squiggled characters on the teleprompter rearranged themselves into words. Somehow she spoke them, wooden, stilted, expecting any moment to see frantic hand signals from the production crew up in the booth. . . .

Then it was over, the music cues up, the cameras dollying back, and she jumped up at the very instant the camera lights went out.

"Good show, Paula."

"Right on, babe."

"Nally wants to see you in the booth."

"Tell Nally he'll have to wait. I have—I have to leave."

Numb, she hesitated briefly in the parking lot. She wanted to drive right up to Seaview. But maybe she should call—try to reach Ted. Maybe it was all a mistake. . . .

• • •

The light on the answering machine in her apartment was blinking. She stared at it from the doorway, then walked over slowly, hit the playback button, and listened in the darkness.

"Paula, it's Betsy. Your dresses are ready. You can pick them up anytime. . . ."

"Hi, Paula, John Sanderson. Let's get together for lunch. . . ."

A pause. . . . "Paula it's me, Ted. . . . I don't know how to tell you. . . . Belinda, she—" His voice broke. "Oh, God, Paula, please call."

Stunned, she stood in the darkened living room, listening to the sounds of her machine. Ted's voice had made it real, and she didn't know what to do. She sat heavily on the arm of a sofa and images of Belinda came unbidden: Belinda at twelve, dark hair in a ponytail, bouncing gleefully on her bed . . . Belinda in high school, shy, pretty, certain she would never be in love . . . Belinda at twenty-one, quiet, competent, and always there for Paula.

Shuddering, she turned on the lamp by the sofa and dialed Ted's number. She let it ring and ring, but there was no answer and the machine didn't come on. Where was he? Suddenly Paula was angry. *Who* killed Belinda? Why? The police were calling it a sex crime. A sex crime! God! Dear, gentle Belinda . . .

She went to the bedroom to throw some things in a bag and stopped at the sight of the bear—the big, overstuffed Winnie the Pooh that Lissa had wanted so badly, and that Belinda had agreed, only days ago, that Paula could safely buy for her birthday without fear of spoiling her.

"I can hardly wait till you get up here, Paula!" She could hear Belinda's voice. *"There's a lot going on, and Ted—oh, well, I need to talk to you, that's all."*

"Is something wrong?"

The slightest pause. *"Yes, I guess you could say that."*

"Between you and Ted?"

Another pause. *"Well—yes. But it's nothing I want to talk about on the phone. Anyway, we'll have all weekend, Paula. I'm really looking forward to it! And wear something smashing for Lissa's party, will you? This time, you're going to meet my boss!"*

It was just like Belinda to be concerned about matchmaking even when something was bothering her. Tears came, and Paula buried her face in the soft plush of the Pooh Bear, hugging it fiercely until the sobs subsided and she felt she could get up and move.

It was a two-hour drive. She thought about the station. . . . Well, she would call them tomorrow. She had planned to go to Seaview, and there was no broadcast on Saturday, anyway. As for Monday, she couldn't worry about that. Maybe she'd be back. Maybe not. . . .

She was throwing some things into a small bag when the thought first occurred to her. *Very likely it would all surface, in spite of everything they'd done. Now, after all these years, the past would come back to haunt her. . . .*

Pressing her lips together, she zipped the bag closed and threw it over her shoulder. She was about to reach for Lissa's bear when the phone rang and she raced to answer it.

"Yes," she said. "Hello! Ted?"

Nothing.

"Ted, is that you?"

A voice whispered into the silence. "Stay . . . away . . . from Seaview."

CHAPTER

2

Paula held the receiver away and stared at it as though it were live, though she'd clearly heard the decisive click as the call was disconnected.

She had to have heard wrong. It made no sense. Why would someone tell her to stay away? Frowning, she hit the button and waited for a dial tone, then hastily punched in Ted's number.

This time it was busy. She could wait and try again. Or she could just get on the road. At this time of night it was a two-hour drive—less, if she broke every speed law.

Pressing her lips together, she glanced around her, as though to prove to herself that everything was as it should be. Then she slung the overnighter over her shoulder along with her leather handbag and balanced the Pooh Bear with her left arm as she locked the front door and pulled it shut.

The wind had died down and it was warm for January, but Paula felt a chill. She threw her overnighter into the trunk of the Honda and rummaged around for an old windbreaker. Then she settled Pooh in the backseat and slipped behind the wheel.

Mist swirled in the light from her headlamps. The coast route would be socked in with fog. Anyway, she could make better time driving inland. She turned up Park Presidio toward the bridge.

On another night she might have stopped to appreciate the glow of the Palace of Fine Arts, the perfect symmetry of the bright lights on the towers of the Golden Gate Bridge. But tonight she saw fragmented pictures of Belinda, at six, at ten, at seventeen—then at twenty-one, on that fateful night before their college graduation; that cool spring night when the whole world was theirs, to reach for and shape to their will.

Blinking, she peered through the thickening mist and tried to concentrate on her driving.

Detective Harvey Nattlinger rubbed the mole on his chin and looked at the boy-man across from him.

He was a hulking youth, maybe five-ten, one-eighty, who said he was twenty-two or twenty-three. He wasn't sure, and from what Nattlinger could see, he could be five years younger—or five years older.

All he knew for certain was that his name was Danny. That, the kid was sure of. Danny One-Eye is what he called himself. It was the only last name he could come up with, and Nattlinger was hard pressed to figure that one out, since the kid appeared to have two normal eyes—normal, that is, unless you considered that slightly vacant gaze of his, a kind of wide-eyed stare that seemed to emanate from some vague and dimly lit place.

And now, of course, his eyes were red. Jeez, the

kid had blubbered buckets! It'd been fully two hours before he'd stopped sobbing long enough to talk to Nattlinger at all.

He'd been cleaned up a little, though his Raiders sweatshirt still bore smears of blood—presumably the blood of the dead woman, Belinda Raymond, since the kid had been at her side when the husband found her.

Nattlinger sat up straighter in his chair and reached across the desk for Garza's report—a prelim scrawled in an uphill slant describing the crime scene in the kitchen.

The swivel chair squeaked, and the kid jerked up, as though he'd forgotten anyone else was in the room. Something like recognition seemed to pass across his face, and then he started crying again.

"I killed her," he wailed, his beefy shoulders heaving. "I diddin' mean to, but I did. She just—she just—she wouldn't wake up. . . ." His voice seemed to catch in his throat, and the next thing Nattlinger knew, the kid was hunched over the desk again, blubbering into his sleeves.

"Ah, hell," Nattlinger muttered, looking out at the clock in the squad room. This thing was going nowhere. The kid had been Mirandized hours ago, and this was as far as they had come. And anyway, there was some niggling doubt in his mind over whether the Miranda would stick. Any public defender worth a rusty dime could argue that the kid didn't understand it.

"Listen"—Nattlinger heaved himself out of the swivel chair—"the both of us could use a little shut-eye. Soon, you'll have yourself a lawyer, maybe calm down a little, too. Maybe then you can tell me what happened. Whaddya think about that?"

The kid appeared not to have heard. His sobs had subsided again. He began to croon. "Diddinmeanit, diddinmeanit. . . ."

Nattlinger shook his head.

It occurred to Paula five miles out of Seaview that it was nearly one in the morning. Ted didn't know for sure she was coming. Suppose he had gone to bed. . . .

Then she groaned. He would hardly be asleep, not after—*Oh, God. Belinda.* Paula clamped her jaws together and picked up speed. She could see the lights of Seaview ahead.

And then she was there, on Rutledge Avenue, in front of the Raymonds' house, the neat split-level with a red brick walkway not five miles from where they'd grown up.

She'd half expected to find a media circus. It was the one part of her job she hated; thrusting a microphone in front of a grief-stricken face was, at best, a gross invasion of privacy.

But it was quiet. Two cars stood side by side in the driveway, and lights blazed from every room. On the surface, everything seemed to be normal. Paula cut the engine and closed her eyes, imagining for a minute that Belinda herself would come running out of the house, Lissa right behind her, peering into the car, wondering what Paula had brought.

She opened the car door. It was midnight quiet. She could hear the crickets, smell the grass. She shuddered, aware of her own heartbeat. *Belinda, can you really be gone?*

Finally she forced herself to move up the walkway. She rang the doorbell and waited. A tall man opened the door a sliver. Paula did not know him.

"Oh, I'm Paula Carroll." She tried to look past him. "Ted—I think—is he home?"

"Paula, of course." The door opened wider. "Sorry to be so cautious. It was a zoo out there earlier— reporters and all. I thought—never mind. Come on in." He held out a hand. "Sam Pierce, Paula. Ted will be glad you're here."

The hand was warm and the grip firm. She looked up at its owner. His face looked tired, but it was a nice face. What was the name he'd said . . . ?

"I'm sorry." He seemed to read her mind. "Belinda worked for me. Sam Pierce."

"Yes," she said, stepping into the hall. "Of course. Belinda talked about you."

He started to say something, then stepped aside, and Paula turned toward the living room.

Ted was bent forward in his chair near the fireplace, his face buried in his hands. If he'd heard them talking, he gave no sign of it. Paula moved forward and cleared her throat.

"Ted . . ."

He looked up, his pale blue eyes startled, and she watched his strong face crumple, as though the very sight of his wife's best friend made it all right for him to cry. "Oh, God," he whispered. "Paula, she's gone. Belinda's—"

"I know. I know." She held out her arms, and he stood up slowly and stumbled into them. They held each other for a long moment until Paula felt awkward and pulled away.

Ted, whom Paula had always regarded as one of the handsomest men she knew, looked haggard and pale, a sort of ashy gray, and older than his thirty years.

"It was awful, Paula." He ran his hands across his face. "God, there was so much blood—"

Shivering, Paula looked toward the kitchen, where Deirdre had said the body had been found.

"They cleaned it up." Ted lowered himself into a chair. "They measured everything and, I don't know, they took about a million pictures, and then they . . . took her . . . took Belinda away, and . . . somebody cleaned it up. . . ."

Paula knelt in front of him and tried to find her voice. "God, it's like a horrible nightmare. I keep expecting to wake up any minute and find out I was dreaming."

Ted caught his breath, a long, shuddering sound. He couldn't seem to find words. In the silence Paula heard her name, and she remembered Sam Pierce's presence.

"I've turned down the lights," he told her softly. "Most of them anyway, and I locked the garage. If there's anything else . . . if I can do anything else . . ." His gray eyes looked earnest and tired.

Paula looked at Ted, who seemed to be staring into space, then she stood and turned toward Sam. "Thank you," she said. "For everything you've done—for staying until I got here. . . ."

She felt awkward again, uttering inane words as though she were the lady of the house. And yet, clearly this man had done what he could, had remained here till one in the morning—this man Belinda had wanted her to meet and now would never introduce her to. . . .

"Look," Sam began, for the second time as though he were reading Paula's mind. "I felt—I mean, it was the least I could do. I haven't known Belinda—or Ted—that long. But in the time I've known them, we've become . . . friends. Good friends. Ted can tell you that."

Paula nodded, touched by his earnestness, by his obvious sensitivity. She swallowed over the lump in her throat. "Yes. I'm sure he will." She glanced back at Ted, then toward the stairway. "Where's Lissa?" she mouthed silently.

"In bed," Sam whispered. "Asleep, I'm sure. The doctor gave her a sedative." He paused. "She knows, but—well, she's only four. . . ."

"I know. Tomorrow is her birthday. . . ." Paula felt the sudden rush of tears. "I'm sorry." She managed to stifle a sob. "I'll be all right in a minute."

She felt Sam Pierce's hand at her elbow. She brushed away the tears. "Thanks. Again." She turned back to him. "We're all—we're going to be fine. It's very late." She gestured toward Ted. "Did the doctor—give him something, too?"

Sam nodded. "He took a second pill just before you got here. That's probably why he seems so . . . zoned out. Would you like—I could help him get upstairs."

Ted was now sprawled back in his chair, his head lolling on the headrest. He looked as though he were already asleep—and fairly comfortably at that.

Paula shook her head. "Let's let him be. If we move him, he may just wake up again. Lord knows he'll need all the rest he can get, just to—get through the day."

Sam nodded again, his generous mouth relaxing into a wan smile. "Yes. We all will. It's going to be hell. God, it already is."

Paula's brain spun with questions. Suddenly she wanted to know it all. When it happened, how it happened, how much of a struggle there'd been—

and this man, this man the police had in custody. Why? Why did he do it?

But it was very late, and though her mind was alert, her whole body seemed to ache. Sam was moving toward the door. She saw him out and locked the door behind him.

Now the silence was almost palpable. She heard the ticking of a clock. Probably in the kitchen. She looked toward it, but couldn't bring herself to go in. The cheery warmth of Belinda's old-fashioned living room was almost more than she could bear.

Ted began snoring softly. He seemed to be deeply asleep. Paula covered him with an afghan from the sofa and turned off the lamp beside his chair.

Her overnight bag was still in her car, but she was suddenly too tired to care. She would stretch out in her clothes in the guest bedroom. She doubted she would sleep much, anyway.

At the top of the stairs she turned to the right. The door to Lissa's bedroom was closed. Slowly, soundlessly, she turned the doorknob and peered into the room.

In the faded moonlight filtering through the curtains, she could just make out Lissa's form. She was lying on her side, facing away, her face not visible from the doorway. Paula felt the sting of tears again, the sobs rising in her throat. She closed the door and hurried down the hall to the room she always used when she was here.

In the half-light she felt for the peach-colored chair that sat to one side of the bed, and sank gratefully into its velvet softness, kicking off her shoes.

As her eyes grew accustomed to the darkness, she recognized the antique dresser, the tester bed with its Quaker lace coverlet, the pleated shade on the bedside lamp.

"I hate fussy," she heard Belinda say, and she jumped at the sound of the voice. *"But there's something so comfortably homey about lace. It's right for the guest room, don't you think? Not that you're a guest, Paula,"* she could hear Belinda's laugh. *"Of course, you're part of the family. But even you could use a little fussing. You don't take very good care of yourself."*

The words were as clear as if they'd just been spoken, as if Belinda were in the room. They seemed to echo in Paula's ears. She hugged herself tightly and cried.

After a while, she sighed raggedly and reached for a tissue from the nightstand. Then she tucked her stockinged feet up under her and settled back in the chair, allowing herself to replay the tapes of a thousand thoughts and memories.

Sleep tugged at her, but something else bobbed just below the surface of her consciousness. She tried to reach for it, but the harder she tried, the more it eluded her grasp. . . .

A scream pierced the thin veil of sleep and brought her, gasping, to her feet.

"Mommeeeee!" The keening wail seemed to shake the floor under her feet.

Her heart pounding, blinded by the darkness, Paula began to run, bumping hard into a table in the hall, vaguely cognizant of pain.

Lissa was sitting up in bed, her little hands over her ears, her eyes wide, screaming, screaming, "Mommy! Mommy! Mommy!"

CHAPTER

3

Felipe Garza was tall and dark, a regular Emilio Estevez. He glared at Nattlinger with smoldering eyes, not a glossy hair out of place.

"You should have been there," he told Nattlinger. "There isn't a doubt in my mind, and when you see the lab reports—I'm telling you, Harve—there won't be any doubt in yours either."

"Tell me again."

"It's all in my report."

"I know. Tell me again."

Garza ran a hand across his olive-skinned face as though to underscore his patience, then shot up out of his chair and began to pace the dingy, yellow-gray office. "We responded to a call from the victim's husband. When we got there, the front door was open. The husband was on the telephone, asking a neighbor to keep ahold of his kid—you know what I mean, to keep her away, not to let her come home yet."

Nattlinger nodded.

"We found the victim on the kitchen floor. Looked like buckets of blood. The suspect, this Danny, was hunched over her. The knife was still in his hand."

He paused, but Nattlinger was not impressed. "Then what happened, Garza?"

"Rattigan ordered the suspect to freeze. I knelt down and felt for the victim's pulse. I couldn't find one. I said I thought she was dead. The suspect started to cry."

Nattlinger waited.

Garza took his time. "I asked the suspect what happened. The first thing he said was, 'Belinda's dead. The knife. The knife. I did it.'"

Nattlinger grimaced. "You may have noticed, Garza, this kid is, shall we say, a couple of six-packs short of a party. What about the husband? You talk to him?"

"Yeah, we talked to him. No way he did her. He's in shock and his whereabouts check out, till he comes home and finds this bonzo moaning over his wife's body. Listen, Nattlinger"—Garza leaned on the desk and flashed his pearly whites—"I'm telling you, man, this is open and shut. The kid said he did it, and he did. The murder weapon is full of his prints— and the neighbors say he had a thing for the victim—followed her around all the time."

Nattlinger looked up. "When'd you get that?"

A slow smile spread across Garza's face. "This morning. Whadja think, I'd just let it go? I talked to the neighbors again."

"Anybody see something?"

Garza shook his head. "But they all know the suspect, Danny One-Eye. They don't know where he lives, but he hangs around the neighborhood. A lot of the kids are scared of him. The victim would let him work around her house. She frequently fed him, they say."

Nattlinger nodded. "Right, I see. The woman was a friend. She fed him. So he turns around and stabs her ten times. Makes all kinds of sense to me."

Garza flushed through his deep tan. "I'm telling you, the kid had a thing for her. Some of the neighbors even teased her about it. So yesterday he comes on to her, and she backs away, and he has some kind of jealous snit."

"A jealous snit."

"Yeah, Harvey, like any other guy who gets the brush. Motive. Weapon. Opportunity. It all adds up to me. He's gonna be arraigned, and I'm telling you, Harve, we're gonna make the charges stick."

Nattlinger rubbed the mole on his chin. *Supercilious little prick.* "Yeah, well, we're running his prints right now. And the lab reports'll be in later."

Garza flushed again. "Well, you know where I am. And thanks for the vote of confidence." He glared at Nattlinger, then turned on his heel and headed out into the squad room.

Nattlinger shifted his burly frame. He'd lied. He'd already run the prints. They had come back clean as a whistle. The suspect—Danny One-Eye, if that was his name—had not been arrested before, not in the state of California anyway, not as Danny One-Eye or anyone else.

Not that it told the whole story. The kid could certainly have done it. Chances were his prints would be the only ones that showed up on the murder weapon.

Through the grimy glass of his windowed office, he could see Garza in the squad room, strutting around, flashing teeth, reeking charm like some guys reek sweat.

Well, maybe Garza was right. The kid did it and that's that. The woman shines him on and he blows his cool. But one thing was certain. This Danny One-Eye was clearly not right in the head. Even if Garza had it right, even if the kid was guilty, he needed to understand the charges against him. If he didn't, Nattlinger knew, there was every chance they could compromise the whole damn case.

The big detective swiveled noisily and reached for the phone. Sometimes the D.A. worked Saturday mornings. What would be the harm in suggesting— informally—that the suspect needed representation? Even before his arraignment Monday. A precaution. Keep everything legit.

Paula had awakened in a tangle of sheets, an odd weight on her chest.

The weight had turned out to be a damp, curly head—Lissa's—cuddled against her, and Paula's heart turned over at the sight, and the feel, of that fragile, little body.

Now Lissa woke as Paula watched her, long, dark lashes fluttering for a hairsbreadth against milk-white, blue-veined skin. Then the azure eyes opened wide. "Paula! Paula! You're here!" Lissa's voice trilled with delight. "You're here! You came for my birthday!"

Paula smoothed back the child's unruly curls. "Well, of course, I did, silly! You knew I would!"

Lissa seemed to have no recollection of her night-mares the night before, of Paula and Ted practically colliding as they rushed to her darkened bedside, of

Paula insisting she would stay with Lissa so Ted could get some rest.

"Look!" Lissa thrust up a chubby little arm. "See what Sam gave me?"

Paula inspected the dainty bracelet that dangled from Lissa's wrist, a twist of gold set with tiny gold hearts at intervals all around. "Oh, Lissa, it's beautiful," she cooed. "Perfect for a pretty little girl. A wonderful little girl who's four years old! My, it's hard to believe!"

With lightning speed the child's smile faded and her lower lip began to quiver. "I wanted a Winnie Pooh cake." Her voice was a whisper. "Mommy said she'd make it." Tears glistened in the corners of her eyes. "But Daddy said"—she swallowed hard—"D— Daddy told me Mommy can't do it. Something bad happened to her, and she won't even be here for my party. . . ."

Lissa looked up through fat, round tears, her expression puzzled but trusting, as though she were positive that somehow Paula could explain this awful mystery.

Paula's heart turned over, and she struggled mightily against the sting of her own tears. Before she could answer, she heard Ted's voice, the sound of his knuckles against the door.

"Anybody up?" he asked softly.

Lissa swallowed again. "Uh-huh."

"Well, good," Ted said, his voice overly hearty. He opened the door halfway.

He was dressed in duck pants and a light cotton sweater, and his face was clean-shaven—pale, but certainly with more color than he'd had the night before. The expression in his eyes told Paula clearly that he planned to act as normal as possible.

"Well, sleepyhead." He moved toward Lissa, chucked her under the chin. "How would you like some cereal, eh? In fact, I've got an idea. You and I can set the table, and Paula can sleep some more if she wants to."

"No," Paula had answered quickly, surprised that she'd slept at all. "I'm awake. My bag. I left it in the trunk. I just want a quick shower."

"No problem. I'll get it." Ted helped Lissa into a quilted lavender robe. "There were a couple of reporters out there this morning, but I think they finally gave up."

Paula nodded, surprised only that they'd given up and left. Though she hated to admit it, most reporters she knew were tenacious enough to hang around all day if it might mean a new angle on a lurid crime or a statement from the newly bereaved.

"The keys are in my purse," she told Ted. "It's downstairs somewhere."

"Right. It'll just take a minute."

Ted hustled Lissa out of the room, and Paula sank into the pillows, incredulous that any of them had been able to sleep in this house at all last night.

Stretching to flex her aching muscles, she heard Lissa's piping voice, and she pondered how you explained death to an innocent, trusting child—how you explained why the light had gone out at the very center of her world. . . .

She jumped at the sudden rap at the door, the thunk of her bag against the floor. She would take her lead from Ted. He was trying hard to be brave in front of Lissa. She got out of bed, retrieved her bag, and headed into the bathroom.

She was rinsing out her contact lenses when a long-forgotten image came to mind—herself at six, a towheaded tomboy with a stubborn streak as long as her arm, furious because the doctor had told her she was nearsighted and was going to have to wear glasses.

"No!" the little tyrant Paula had screeched. "No! I won't! I won't!" And her mother had listened calmly and turned on her heel and walked out of the room.

A day or two later Paula'd answered the doorbell, and there was Belinda on the porch—her dark hair neatly tied back in braids and eyeglasses perched on her nose.

Dumbfounded, Paula had asked to try them on, decided they were kind of fun, and agreed that maybe it wasn't so awful to have to wear glasses after all.

Paula smiled, putting in her contacts. It had been months before she'd realized she'd been tricked. Belinda's eyes were perfectly fine. Her spectacles were only clear glass, purchased by Paula's mother for docile Belinda for exactly the purpose they'd served!

Oh, Belinda! Paula steadied herself a minute against the cool, tiled counter. Then she hastily pulled on a shirt and denim skirt and started down the stairs.

She could hear Lissa's voice before she rounded the corner. Ted had chosen to have breakfast in the dining room. She closed her eyes and wondered if they would ever again be comfortable in this kitchen—in this house.

She pulled out a chair next to Lissa's, where a place had been set for her, and she tried to sound cheerful despite the gloom that threatened to settle around them.

Ted jumped up. "I'll get you some coffee."

"Thanks," she heard herself say, a part of her wanting to go into the kitchen and another part of her dreading it.

"Paula." Lissa was tugging at her arm. "Are you going to have Cheerios, like me?"

Paula wasn't hungry, but she reached for the box. "Yum! Of course, I am! Cheerios! And then, maybe we'll go out to my car and see what there is for your birthday."

"In your car?" Lissa's blue eyes shone. "My birthday present is in your car?"

"Could be." Paula poured milk on the cereal. "But first you have to finish breakfast."

Lissa was watching her. "Paula," she piped, "how come you pour milk with *that* hand? Mommy does it with *this* one!" She held up her right hand. "Mommy does *everything* with this one."

Paula smiled. How could she explain the vagaries of left-handedness and right-handedness—that the world wasn't made for left-handed people, but that somehow they managed to adjust?

"Well," she said finally, "everybody is born with two hands and two feet. But as you grow up, you find that some things—like eating and writing—are easier to do with one hand than the other." She held out a spoon. "Here, take this, sweetheart."

Lissa reached for it with her right hand.

"See?" Paula said. "You reached out with your right hand. That means you're probably right-handed."

Lissa looked down and inspected her hands, as though she were making a decision.

Paula smiled. "Use the one that's easier. One is just as good as the other."

Lissa grinned, picked up her spoon, and began to eat her cereal.

Ted had not returned with the coffee, and Paula began to get uneasy. She tried to peer through the half-open kitchen door as Lissa chattered away.

"There!" Lissa said finally, pushing her bowl away. "I'm all done. Now can we go and see what's out in your car?"

Paula hesitated. "In a minute, yes. But look! You don't have any slippers on. It's damp outside, and you're barefooted. Run upstairs and get your slippers."

Lissa slid down out of her chair and scooted around the corner. When Paula could hear her footsteps on the stairs, she steeled herself and went into the kitchen.

It was clean and white, the way Paula remembered it. There was no sign of any struggle. Ted was standing, staring at the coffeepot, arms quietly at his sides.

"She's gone, Paula." His voice was toneless. "God, I miss her already."

Paula hesitated. "This . . . man they've arrested. He was here, in your kitchen. Who is he?"

"Danny? You've probably met him yourself. You know, that kid who . . . hangs around a lot. Big kid, not quite right in the head. He was always mooning around Belinda."

"Mooning around—" Paula stopped, unbelieving. "Danny! He called himself Danny One-Eye!"

Ted whirled around to face her, his eyes an ominous blue-gray. "That's him. Danny One-Eye. That dim-witted bastard. He did it! He killed Belinda!"

"Ted—"

"He did it! He told me he did it. He told the police

he did, too! He ate my food. He played with my child. I *told* Belinda he was dangerous. . . ."

Paula tried to picture the hulking youth. She had seen him once or twice, raking leaves, carrying trash, doing whatever Belinda asked.

"Belinda wouldn't listen. He was gentle, she said! He wouldn't hurt a fly!" Ted's voice was a hiss. "Well, she was wrong, dead wrong! I hope they string him up by his balls!"

CHAPTER

—4—

Mike Shaffer tore the perforated edges off the computer paper, whacked the stacked pages on his desktop to straighten them, and stowed them neatly in his briefcase. Then he signed off the computer, took a gulp of cold coffee, and looked out the office window.

The early morning fog had burned off, and a wash of pale sunlight gave the stuccoed buildings of downtown Seaview an almost buttery cast. He'd known these buildings for most of his life, and he liked being part of their routine. But now he was mad at himself for coming in on Saturday, for being here when the D.A. had called, and he stared sullenly at the low-slung, stucco box that housed the police station and the jail.

"So much for the quick print, the haircut, and the picnic," he ran a hand through sandy-colored hair. It was past eleven now. By the time he got through at the city jail, the day was going to be half shot.

On the other hand, he was amazed to realize he

didn't mind at all calling Gloria. She was nice enough, but his day wouldn't be ruined if he didn't get to spend it with her.

"Gloria, it's Mike." He tried to sound harried. "I called as soon as I knew. There's some kid sitting in jail, and I was here in the office when the D.A. called and asked me to go see him. Kid's in on a murder charge, and—what? Yeah. . . . I'm sorry. I'm going to have to cancel."

He listened to Gloria letting him off the hook, and it almost struck him as funny. She was saying the right things, but if she was really disappointed, she was doing a good job of hiding it.

"Thanks for understanding." He reached for his jacket. "Defender of the masses and all that . . ." Then he was off the phone, and he picked up his briefcase and smiled at the satisfying heft of it.

He took the stairs two at a time, his jacket slung over his shoulder. It was warm for January, and by the time he reached the jail, he could feel the perspiration on his back. "Yo, Dickie." He grinned at Officer Richard Hetherington. "Helluva way to spend a weekend."

Hetherington smiled sourly. "I don't notice you out golfin' on the back nine."

Mike shrugged. "What can I tell you? Curse of the class of '84. We're a little heavy on the work ethic. But what the hell, we'll fool 'em all. We'll retire early—and rich."

"Yeah, right." Dickie Hetherington pushed his affable features into something resembling a snarl. "I'll remember you said that when I'm buyin' beans on my generous public-service pension." His features rearranged themselves. "You heard about Belinda? Speakin' of the class of '84."

Mike frowned. "Belinda?"

"Belinda Raymond. Used to be Belinda Talmadge.
She hung around with Paula. Paula Carroll. Don't
tell me you don't remember her."

"Belinda, sure." Mike pictured the face. Sweet. A
pretty brunette. He hadn't seen her—or Paula, for
that matter, since they'd all gone off to college.

"Well, she's dead. Murdered."

"Belinda Talmadge?"

"Raymond. She was murdered. Yesterday. We got
the suspect in custody. A real creep. A naggie, is what
I hear."

Naggie. Jargon for a street person—somebody
who nagged you for handouts. "Ah, hell." Mike sat on
the corner of the intake desk. "Don't tell me. His
name is Danny—something."

"One-Eye." Dickie peered at him. "That's what he
says. Oh, man. Don't tell me you're defending him."

"By personal invitation of the district attorney.
Prior to arraignment yet."

Dickie shook his head. "Good luck on this one. Kid
don't even deny it."

Mike shrugged. "Who brought him in?"

"Garza."

"Got a report?"

"Prelim, yeah. Hold on, I'll get you what we got."

Dickie got up, tucked his shirt into his pants, and
ambled toward a file cabinet.

Mike sat on a corner of the desk and remembered
Paula Carroll. Willowy. Golden. Untouchable Paula.
Jeez, he hadn't thought of her in years. And Belinda.
Yes, he remembered her, too. Dead. God, what a
world.

Dickie brought back a thin sheaf of papers and
held them out with a flourish.

"Thanks." Mike got up off the edge of the desk and moved to an orange plastic chair. He tossed his jacket on the one next to it and sat down to read the report.

Lissa was standing in the kitchen doorway, clutching the giant Pooh Bear. But she wasn't smiling. She was staring at her father, her blue eyes dark with pain.

"Well, look here!" Paula forced brightness into her voice. "You went out to my car without me. And look what you found! Happy birthday, sweetheart. Ted, look what Lissa's found!"

Ted seemed to draw himself up and make an effort to smile. "Oh, my gosh. Will you look at that! He's bigger than you are, hon! What do you say to Paula? Come on, sweetheart. Give her a great big hug!"

Lissa tried to smile, but her lower lip quivered. She looked so totally forlorn. Paula swallowed hard over the lump in her throat. Then she knelt and held out her arms.

In a minute they were filled with lavender satin and fuzzy bear and warm, childish flesh, and it took every ounce of willpower she had to keep from bursting into tears. She rocked slowly back and forth until she felt the child begin to squirm. Then she released her and leaned on one knee and tried out a shaky smile.

"Mommy likes Pooh Bear, too," Lissa murmured. "She can't come back. Daddy said . . ." She looked at Ted. "Does she know I have him? Can she see my brand-new Pooh?"

Paula wondered how long Lissa'd stood in the doorway; how much of Ted's diatribe she'd heard. One thing was certain. She was going to suggest that Lissa see a child psychologist—someone who could help her understand her feelings in a way neither she or Ted could.

To his credit, Ted kept his voice steady. "I bet Mommy knows about Pooh. And I know she wants you to have a happy birthday even if she can't be here."

Paula regarded him with a strange mixture of admiration and wonder, glad he was able to deal with Lissa, but amazed at how . . . detached he seemed to be—at how much he even looked like his old self, recovered from his pallor of the night before.

She shook her head at the disloyal thought. Only moments ago he'd been grieving for Belinda. He was doing his best to keep his composure in front of Lissa. She could certainly appreciate that.

"Hello! Anyone home?"

Paula jumped at the sound.

"Sam," Ted called. "We're in here!"

Paula brought herself to a standing position as Sam Pierce strode into the room.

"Well, good morning." He scooped up Lissa, giant Pooh Bear and all. "And what, pray tell, is this monstrous bear who seems to have wandered into your kitchen?"

Lissa giggled. "It's Pooh, silly! Paula brought him for my birthday. Didn't you, Paula? Tell Sam. Say, 'Sam, this is Lissa's Pooh Bear!'"

In the morning light, and having had some sleep, Sam Pierce was disarmingly good-looking—better even than Belinda had suggested all those months when she'd wanted them to meet.

"Sam, this is Lissa's Pooh Bear," she said, mimicking Lissa's tone. "He's come to live with her and tell her stories about Piglet and Roo and Eeyore."

"Really?" She saw the hint of amusement in Sam's steady, gray eyes, the ready crinkle of little laugh lines in an otherwise unlined face. "And here I thought he was Brer Bear, just coming in out of the cornfield!"

That sent Lissa into peals of laughter. "Brer Bear wears a hat!"

Paula marveled at the child's resilience. Did she feel as carefree as she sounded? Would any of them ever be so carefree again, now that Belinda was gone?

Sam winked at Paula, as though he'd read her mind. "Well"—he ruffled Lissa's curls—"I thought maybe I could keep Lissa company if—well, in case you have . . . things to do."

Ted seemed to understand immediately. "Thanks, Sam. I was going to ask a neighbor . . ."

Paula closed her eyes, comprehending at last. Of course. Arrangements . . . had to be made. "Ted"—she looked at him—"do you want—shall I go with you?"

He nodded. "If you would. I'd appreciate it."

She glanced once around the sunny kitchen, empty somehow despite their presence. She could almost see Belinda, sitting at the breakfast bar, chewing on the end of a pencil, writing out a grocery list in her neat, precise hand, asking how they felt about barbecue. . . .

"Of course." Paula looked from one to the other. "Come, Lissa. Let's go and change clothes. And while we're at it, we'll find some of your Pooh books for Sam to read to you while we're gone."

The cell walls were the same buttery color as the stucco on the outside of the building, but there was little natural light in the center of the box. The walls seemed a pasty gray.

The suspect was hunched forward on the edge of his cot, a big, hulking youth, his dark, stubbled chin resting, childlike, in his large, meaty hands. He did not look up when Mike entered the cell or when he cleared his throat audibly.

"Danny." His voice seemed unnaturally loud but the kid only looked up and blinked. Mike held out a hand. "I'm Mike Shaffer. I'm a lawyer. A public defender."

The kid blinked again, but his eyes seemed vacant, and although he glanced at the extended hand, he made no move to shake it.

"Do you know that you are in jail, Danny? That you may be in serious trouble?"

The youth nodded. "Belinda's dead. . . . I know . . . Belinda's dead."

Mike paused. "Did you tell the police you killed her?"

A nod.

"Did you kill her?"

A shrug.

Mike waited. When the kid said nothing, he cleared his throat again. "Do you remember my name?"

"Mike."

"Right. I'm a lawyer. And your name is—"

"Danny."

"Danny what?"

"Danny One-Eye."

"One . . . eye? Are you saying 'one eye'?" He enunciated the words carefully.

Danny nodded. Mike looked at him puzzled. The kid seemed to have two good eyes. Dull, yes, but they both seemed to function, at least as far as Mike could tell. He decided to try again. "Do you have another name, Danny? Another last name? Besides One-Eye?"

The kid shrugged his massive shoulders. "One-Eye. Danny One-Eye."

Mike sat down on the only chair in the cell. Where would the kid get a name like that? One-Eye. . . . Somehow, he doubted that was it, but he couldn't think of a surname it sounded like.

He tried another tack. "Where do you live, Danny?"

The youth shrugged again.

"In Seaview?"

"Seaview."

"Did you grow up in Seaview? Where did you go to school?"

"I don't know . . . Rock."

"Rock? Did you say 'rock'?"

Danny blinked, as though he'd forgotten Mike was there. "Where's Lissa? Happy birthday. . . ." Tears welled in his dull brown eyes. "Belinda. I hurt Belinda. . . ."

It was the most animated the kid had been, the most words he'd said at one time. "How did you hurt her?"

"Knife. The knife."

"Where did you get the knife?"

No response. He tried another tack. "Who's Lissa, Danny?" he asked gently.

"Lissa. Birthday."

"Lissa's birthday. How old is Lissa, Danny?"

A loud snuffle.

"Do you know how old? Is Lissa Belinda's daughter?"

Danny turned away. He seemed agitated, as though the concept was more than he could grasp.

"Think, Danny. You went to Belinda's house. Why? For Lissa's birthday?"

"Danny brought . . . balloons." The kid began to moan. "Belinda . . . Belinda's dead. . . ."

"I know. Danny, this is important. Tell me what happened in Belinda's house."

The eyes went blank, the face stony.

Mike uttered a silent oath. The client conference was over.

CHAPTER

—5—

Except for a narrow slice of view from the canyon at the north edge of town, there was simply no way you could see the sea from Seaview. It was a misnomer, and one that Paula had sneered at in the years when she was growing up.

But then, she reflected, watching the landscape go by from the passenger seat of Ted's Buick, she had sneered at a lot of things in those tender years before she'd been away long enough to miss them.

"The Strand is gone!" She turned to look back at the empty lot where the old movie house had been. "And Moon Burgers, too. For heaven's sake, when did all that happen?"

"Two years ago. More. I did the site inspection when the city declared the theater unsafe."

"*Was* it unsafe?"

"Absolutely. The '89 earthquake did it in."

Paula nodded. The '89 quake, which had nearly devastated certain areas of San Francisco, had also left its mark in Seaview. Ted, who did safety inspections for the state, had put in tons of overtime. . . .

"It's awful," Belinda had told Paula in one of their frequent Sunday phone calls. *"Here I am, starting a new job, and Ted is gone twelve or fourteen hours a day—sometimes even overnight!"*

"The good news"—Ted broke into her thoughts—"is that we now have a five-plex at one end of the mall. And they're going to be putting in a minimall here. It's supposed to be called Strand Plaza."

Strand Plaza. Paula grimaced. What the world needed was another minimall! And a brand-new five-plex, with molded plastic seats in a sterile, cement box of a theater!

She smiled in spite of herself, recalling long matinees on Saturday afternoons at the Strand. She and Belinda, munching popcorn, wild about *American Graffiti*. And later, practically swooning over John Travolta in *Saturday Night Fever.* . . .

She closed her eyes. This couldn't be happening. She remembered so much, so clearly . . . the day they'd left the movie theater early when Belinda had suddenly felt sick. By the time they got her home, she was doubled up with pain. A ruptured appendix, the doctor said. Peritonitis. She might have died if they hadn't caught it in time. . . .

Paula moaned. She had felt so bereft when they'd put Belinda into the hospital. How could she stand it on Sunday morning when they put her into the ground?

Mike Shaffer pulled a Greenpeace T-shirt over his head and threw his damp shirt in the hamper. Then he padded into the kitchen, took a beer from the fridge and carried it out to the deck.

In town a pale, insistent sunlight had burned its

way through the fog, but here in the arroyo beyond his minuscule yard, mist hung in the trees like cotton batting. It was cooler, too, and the air was filled with a green, mulchy smell that reminded Mike why he'd stretched to buy this place on the salary the county paid him.

Feeling better, he settled himself in a chair and took a swig of his beer. Then he put his feet up on a battered wooden table and thought about Danny One-Eye.

One-Eye. Wunny. Walmsley. Wondry. The possibilities were endless. How was he supposed to get a bead on the kid when he wasn't even sure of his name? Or his age, for that matter? He agreed with Nattlinger. The kid was probably *somewhere* between eighteen and twenty-five.

According to the report, Danny One-Eye's prints were the only ones on the murder weapon. There was no match in the state's computer, so priors were still an unknown. But it wouldn't be the first time a conviction was made purely on the basis of fingerprint evidence.

Mike shook his head. The kid said he did it, and he seemed to understand why he was in jail. But given his retardation, or whatever was wrong with him, it was easy to see why Nattlinger had opted to cover the department's ass by requesting a public defender from the outset.

Evaluations were going to be needed, probably by a forensic psychologist, but since the prosecution could undoubtedly make a case that Danny was a viable suspect, Mike would have to do some fancy digging if he was going to mount a reasonable defense.

The husband, for one thing. Belinda's husband.

Mike didn't think he knew him. What kind of relationship had he had with his wife? Had he even been asked for an alibi?

Finishing the beer, he went inside to retrieve his notes from his briefcase. He'd feel better if he had some handle on the kid before the arraignment on Monday.

"Nuts," he muttered, putting aside the pages he'd printed out that morning. With luck, he might get to read through them tomorrow and make some notes in the margin.

But he *was* intrigued. His juices were flowing. What was Danny's relationship to Belinda Talmadge? *Raymond*, he corrected himself. Belinda Raymond. What was his relationship to Belinda Raymond? If she was a friend, as the neighbors suggested, then why would he suddenly turn on her?

His own recollection of Belinda was fuzzy—a sweet kid, a shadow to Paula Carroll. He wondered idly if the women had remained friends, if Paula would come home for the funeral. Then he told himself he was an insensitive clod, and he forced himself back on track.

The murder weapon was a good-quality kitchen knife with a sharp, six-inch steel blade. It might have come from the victim's own kitchen, though the husband could not positively identify it. Where else would this allegedly homeless suspect get hold of a knife of that quality? Steal it? Carry it around in his sock? Where did he sleep nights, anyway?

Mike glanced at his notes. The kid seemed to indicate he'd grown up in or near Seaview.

"Where did you go to school?"

"Rock . . ."

Rock. What the hell did that mean?

Hauling the phone book out of a kitchen drawer, he tossed it onto the counter. He grabbed a salted pretzel from an open cellophane bag and, munching, flipped open the book.

There were three school districts in or near Seaview. He checked the listings for all three. There were no schools in any of them called rock-anything, or anything remotely like it.

The pretzels were stale. He grabbed the bag and took it out to the deck. He tossed a few to a couple of squirrels and pondered his next step.

They were silent on the long drive home from the mortuary. For Paula, the mortuary had finally made it real. Belinda was gone, and how she would *hate* it if they crumbled and fell apart in her absence.

Ted had handled things with quiet authority, making decisions as he needed to. But now his profile was chiseled in stone, his chin thrust stubbornly forward, and Paula knew this was not the time to discuss what might happen next. Besides, her own thoughts were still too jumbled, her pain too unbearably fresh, to spend much time thinking about what direction their lives would take.

She stared out at the changing landscape, seeing but only half comprehending it—the auto row at the edge of town, where once there'd been only forest . . . a cinderblock post office perched on a bluff they used to climb down to get to the river.

There was chain-link fencing around the old oil refinery where her father had worked for so many years—and some kind of sign posted just inside the fence, but they were past before she could read it.

She turned toward Ted, but he was looking straight ahead, his jaw firmly clenched—and anyway, they were approaching the last left turn that led to Rutledge Avenue.

"Someone's here," she said, before they were close enough for her to recognize the woman at the front door—a slim brunette who was having some difficulty juggling two bulging grocery bags.

"It's Judy Morrissey." Ted pulled into the driveway. "She's a neighbor, two doors down. She had Lissa with her last night—" He didn't finish the sentence.

The woman turned at the sound of the engine, and Paula nodded, recognizing her. She had met Judy once or twice—and her daughter, Tiffany, a vivacious little thing who was the same age as Lissa.

"Hi." Judy gave them a tentative smile. "I didn't want to disturb you. . . ."

"It's okay," Ted told her. "We're trying to hang in there. Do you know our friend—Paula Carroll?"

Judy nodded in Paula's direction. "Yes, of course. How are you?" She bit her lip. "Stupid question. I feel—oh, God, it still seems so impossible. . . ."

Ted nodded, but Judy didn't wait. She gestured toward the grocery bags. "I brought some things. I thought, well, you're bound to get hungry. It's a ham, and—a few other things."

Ted leaned forward and reached for the doorknob, but Judy put a hand on his arm. "Wait," she said. "Before we go inside, there's something I want to ask."

Paula was touched by the woman's openness, by the lack of pity in her tone. Judy seemed to sense her understanding. She looked from one to the other.

"Look," she said finally, "I hope you don't think I'm awful even to suggest it, but Lissa's only four. And it is her birthday. I'm afraid she won't understand. . . ." She took a deep breath. "Would it be all right if we had her party—at my house?"

The last of the words came out in a rush, but there was no mistaking her intent. Lissa would have to face reality. But she didn't have to do it all at once.

Ted seemed to wrestle with himself, his jaw working silently. Finally he nodded. "I think—maybe Belinda would like that. . . ."

Paula picked up one of the shopping bags and opened the door briskly, as much to get a grip on herself as to get them all inside.

In the living room Sam Pierce looked up from a book, his glasses low on his nose. Lissa, who was curled up close beside him, sighed and tugged at his arm. "What did Pooh say?" she asked loudly, clearly annoyed at the interruption.

Sam looked down. "'I'm hungry,'" he read. "'I think I want some hunny!'"

Smiling despite herself, Paula hefted the shopping bag and headed toward the kitchen, where Judy Morrissey was putting things into the refrigerator while Ted watched in silence.

"So hard to believe," Judy whispered, trying hard not to stare at the floor. "I'm sorry"—two red spots formed on her cheeks—"I promised myself I wouldn't do this."

Paula touched her arm. "I know. We're all just doing the best we can. I think it's really wonderful of you to want to give Lissa her party."

"Ted's right. It's what Belinda would want." Judy wiped away a tear. "Maybe you could help Lissa pick out a party dress while I go home and make a few calls. I'll be back to pick her up in half an hour, if that's all right with you."

Paula looked at Ted, who shrugged distractedly. She nodded. "Yes, of course."

Lissa's eyes lit up when Paula told her she was going to have her party at the Morrisseys'.

"What would you like to wear?" Paula asked her.

"I know!" Lissa led the way upstairs, chattering all the while. "I have new shoes! Did you know I have new shoes? They're black and they're all shiny. Mommy said I could wear them to my party. Can I still, Paula? Please?"

She picked out a pale blue organdy party dress with a frilly white apron over the skirt, and managed—barely—to hold still while Paula helped her with her bath and struggled to tie two slippery hair ribbons into relatively neat little bows.

"There." Paula stepped back to look at her handiwork.

Lissa was staring into the mirror. "Is Danny One-Eye coming to my party?"

Paula was startled. "No, Lissa. Why would he come to your party?"

"Mommy said he could. She said he was our friend. But he isn't. He hurt Mommy."

Paula hesitated. "How do you know that?"

"Daddy said. I heard him."

Of course, he had. And Lissa had been standing just outside the kitchen door. Now she had lost even more than Belinda. She had lost her friend, too.

Paula was dimly aware of a phone ringing. She knelt and gathered Lissa to her. "Lissa, all we know for sure is that something bad happened to Mommy. It's the reason she can't be here with us anymore, the reason she can't be at your party. But she loves you, Lissa. She will always love you. No matter what happens. Do you understand?"

"Paula!"

It was Sam, and it sounded urgent. Lissa nodded solemnly. Giving her another quick hug, Paula headed toward the top of the stairs.

Sam looked up. "Everything okay?"

Paula nodded. "I think so."

"That was the Seaview police on the phone. I'm going downtown with Ted."

Her heart skipped a beat. "What's wrong?" she mouthed, looking back toward Lissa.

Sam came halfway up the stairs and kept his voice low. "I don't know. Maybe something's turned up. The police want to talk to Ted."

CHAPTER

6

"Is my daddy coming back?"

Lissa stood in the doorway, looking out long after Sam's BMW had disappeared around the corner.

Relieved to see no reporters around, Paula ruffled Lissa's hair. "Of course, your daddy's coming back. He'll want to hear all about your party."

It seemed to satisfy her. Lissa closed the door. "Can Pooh come with me to my party?"

"What a good idea!" Paula put her hands on her hips. "Now, where could that bear have gone?"

Lissa giggled and ran to the sofa. "Look! He's right here," she cried, barely managing to reach around his girth and give him a big hug.

Paula understood why Lissa was worried that Ted might not come back. If one parent could be lost to her without warning, then the other one could disappear, too. Lissa's anxiety broke Paula's heart, but it strengthened her resolve to bring up the matter of counseling.

Lissa looked joyful when the doorbell rang. "It's Mrs. Morrissey! It's time for the party!"

She ran to the door and pulled it open, with Paula following right behind. But it wasn't Judy who stood in the doorway. It was a man Paula didn't know.

He was tall and broadly built, about her own age, with longish, sandy-colored hair—and he stood there, staring at her as though he were amazed to see her standing in the doorway.

Wary, she spoke in a measured tone. "Yes? Is there something I can help you with?"

"Paula Carroll." He smiled slightly. "You don't remember me, do you?"

"No—"

"Mike Shaffer. Seaview, '84. We graduated together from high school."

Paula cocked her head, thinking hard. The pleasant, open grin. She had a vague recollection of a football player. She'd turned him down for the prom.

Lissa fidgeted. "There's Mrs. Morrissey!"

Judy was coming up the walk. "Hi! Sorry, I can see you have company. We'll just be on our way."

Lissa looked up. "Can I go now? Please?"

"Of course, you can, honey."

She darted inside and returned seconds later, dragging Pooh by one arm.

Judy reached down and hefted Pooh up. "We'll be just down the street," she told Paula. "And I'll have her back by five o'clock, if that's okay with you."

"Fine." Paula nodded. "Five will be fine. Have fun at the party, Lissa!"

But Lissa was already skipping down the street. Judy waved and took off after her.

Mike Shaffer turned back to Paula. "Cute little girl. Yours?"

Paula thought it was none of his business. "No. Was there something you wanted?"

He looked chagrined. "Sorry," he apologized. "Actually, I came to see Ted Raymond. If he'll see me, that is. I'm the defense attorney who'll be representing Danny One-Eye."

"Danny—" It seemed to take a moment for the meaning of the words to sink in. "You're representing Danny One-Eye. The man who murdered Belinda."

His voice was soft. "Allegedly murdered. He hasn't yet been found guilty."

Paula stared at him. *Allegedly* murdered. Words she might use in a news broadcast. He had his nerve, this Mike Shaffer, coming here to Belinda's house—expecting to talk to the husband of the woman *allegedly* murdered by his client, *allegedly* stabbed again and again, until she bled to death in her kitchen!

He had to have seen the hostility in her face, but if he did, he chose to ignore it. His brown eyes seemed to radiate warmth. "I'm terribly sorry," he said.

Paula felt her breathing quicken. She couldn't seem to find words, and he seemed to take her stunned silence as a signal to go on talking.

"I know Belinda was your friend," he murmured. "I remember that from high school. I know how awful—how horrified you must be, and I want to offer my condolences."

"Your condolences," Paula sputtered finally, her breath lodged somewhere in her throat. "You lowlife, you have the unmitigated gall to offer your *condolences!*"

It was as if, suddenly, everything she'd been

feeling since she'd learned about Belinda's murder—
all the pain, the rage, the bottomless sorrow she'd
subdued in front of Ted and Sam and Lissa—came
spewing out, hot and venomous, relieved to have
found a target.

"What makes you think you know how I feel—that
you have any idea what we've lost? What gives you
the right to offer your *condolences* when you're
defending the scum who said he killed her?"

She became aware that she was pounding on his
chest, keening like a wounded animal. And then, as
suddenly as the rage had peaked, it seemed to drain
away, leaving her empty, cast adrift in some strange
and alien sea.

She let herself be led inside, deposited, shaking,
on the sofa. When her sobs subsided, she looked at
Mike Shaffer and felt color rise in her cheeks.

"I'm sorry," she began. "I had no right—"

He held up a hand. "No, please. You're right—I
can't know how you feel. But I am sorry. I knew
Belinda. She was kind and gentle and sweet."

Paula leaned back deep into her chair. "She was.
She was kind to everyone. I suppose that's why it's
so hard to accept that her life . . . ended with such
violence."

Mike nodded. "I understand. No one should die so
horribly. But the system, for all its aberrations,
trudges along pretty well. The truth will come out.
And when it does, the killer will be convicted."

The cynic in her couldn't be stilled. "Come on,
Mike Shaffer. Tell the truth. How often does the
defense attorney look for legal loopholes, even when
he thinks his client is guilty?"

"About as often as the prosecution goes for the
jugular with nothing but circumstantial evidence."

Paula looked at him. "And what if it turns out that your client *is* the killer? Will it bother you at all that you defended a monster who wasn't worthy of defense?"

"Yes." Mike Shaffer met her gaze. "But it would bother me even more if this retarded kid who can't defend himself takes the rap for somebody else."

"You don't think he did it."

"Too soon to tell."

"He told the police he did."

Mike nodded. "I know. But he doesn't express himself well, and it's hard to understand how he thinks. Belinda was his friend. Why would he kill her? What possible reason could he have?"

Paula tried to picture the lumbering youth she'd seen at the house before. Once, last spring, she and Belinda had been sipping iced tea on the patio. It was a warm day, and Belinda had asked Danny to move the best part of half a cord of firewood. Paula had watched, oddly fascinated by the robotlike quality of his motions as he stacked the logs in meticulous rows to one side of the garage, stopping only to straighten out the string of Lissa's yo-yo with his big, meaty hands.

"*Are you warm, Danny?*" Belinda had called. "*Would you like a glass of iced tea?*"

"*No, ma'am.*" He had tipped a grimy baseball cap, and his smile had been shy and adoring. "*But if it's no problem, Danny One-Eye will sure be ready for some supper.*"

Belinda'd had a pot of spaghetti sauce simmering most of the afternoon. She did not ask Danny to join them for dinner, but she did pack a good-sized supper and hand it to Danny along with a five-dollar bill, which he'd happily stuffed in his pocket.

Paula tried to reconcile the memory of that child-like grin with Ted's vitriolic description of him. It was a little like trying to imagine a bloody cleaver in the hands of one of Santa's elves.

She looked at Mike Shaffer. "What do you mean, he could be taking the rap for someone else?"

Mike shrugged. "A figure of speech. We have yet to reconstruct the murder. When we do—and when we know something more definitive about Danny, any number of scenarios are possible."

"Right." Paula felt the stirrings of impatience. "Some psychopathic slasher broke into Belinda's kitchen, and your client just happened to wander in after the slasher left her for dead."

Mike's gaze was level. "That's one possibility. Another is that it was someone else she knew."

"Someone she knew. Who for God's sake? Who could have hated her that much?"

He held up his hands in a helpless gesture. "Her lover? Her boyfriend? Her husband? You're a news reporter, Paula. Surely you know the husband is the first likely suspect."

Paula came up out of her chair with a rush that left her dizzy. "You're crazy." Her voice was deadly calm. "This conversation is over. Is that what you came to discuss with Ted Raymond? Whether he murdered his wife?"

"I only meant—"

"Get out," she told him, leading the way to the door.

"Paula—"

"Get out." She held the door open and fixed him with an icy stare.

He hesitated briefly, meeting her stare with an uncomprehending expression. Then he turned on his heel, and she slammed the door after him with swift and satisfying force.

She was breathing hard again, trembling with rage. The colossal, unmitigated gall! To come to this house less than twenty-four hours after Belinda was savagely murdered, and imply—no, suggest—that she might have died at the hands of her own husband!

Paula hugged herself and breathed deeply. It was ridiculous to get so upset. Clearly Mike Shaffer's years as a high school lineman had played havoc with his brain.

She looked at her watch. It was just after two. Belinda had not been gone a day. It was incomprehensible that by noon on Sunday she would be laid to her final rest.

Clothing! The service would be closed-casket, but Paula had promised Ted that she would choose the clothes Belinda would be buried in. It was not a chore to which she looked forward, but it was something that had to be done. Steeling herself, she went upstairs and headed for Belinda's closet.

She was not surprised that Belinda's things were neatly hung away, dresses and suits to one side of the closet, blouses above skirts and slacks, shoes stacked on shelves in their original boxes with styles and colors labeled.

The familiar scent of Belinda's cologne brought the sting of tears to Paula's eyes. She could feel Belinda's presence, see her face, hear her voice, as though she were right there in the room.

"Is something wrong?" Paula had asked her.

The slightest pause. *"Yes. I guess you could say that."*

"Between you and Ted?"

Another pause. *"Well—yes. But it's nothing I want to talk about on the phone. . . ."*

Nothing you wanted to talk about on the phone. What was it, Belinda, what? Surely nothing serious—not really serious, not serious enough to lead to murder?

Ridiculous! Paula shook her head, ashamed to have entertained the notion. Her fingers moved from nubby wools to cottons and watered silks.

Her attention was caught by the elegant gowns at one end of the closet, gossamer creations in delicate pastels perfect for Belinda's coloring, and it occurred to Paula that she had no idea where Belinda might have worn them.

Not that it mattered where she wore them, or if she wore them at all. Blinking, Paula forced herself back to the task she'd started in the first place.

Her hand moved to a dress she remembered, a delicate floral print that Belinda had bought when she fell in love with it during a shopping expedition in San Francisco. Now, if she could find some navy pumps. . . . She turned toward shelves of shoes and handbags.

On an upper shelf, between two leather handbags, were several slim, little volumes. Paula reached up and took one down. A diary. 1992. She riffled the pages, her heart turning over at the sight of Belinda's familiar hand. . . .

"Is something wrong?"

The slightest pause. *"Yes. I guess you could say that. . . . "*

Ashamed of her impulse, Paula groaned and slammed the small book shut. She had known Ted for years. Damn Mike Shaffer and his cool insinuation. How could she be so disloyal?

Quickly, she put the book back on the shelf and found the rest of the things she needed. She placed them all in a travel bag, which she left on a chaise in the bedroom.

Relieved to be done with it, she checked her watch again. Scarcely twenty minutes had passed. It would be a while before Judy brought Lissa home, but where were Sam and Ted? What was so urgent that the police had insisted on talking to Ted right away? And what was it that teased at her, that she couldn't bring to mind no matter how hard she tried . . . ?

Edgy, she wandered the silent rooms as though she'd never seen them before, admiring all over again Belinda's knack for combining comfort and beauty. Finally, she ended up in the living room, where she perched on the arm of Ted's recliner and pointed the remote control unit at the television.

A blond reporter with a vacuous expression was teasing the five o'clock news. With a start, Paula realized she had not called her station—or her agent—to tell them where she was.

Silencing the television, she moved to the phone and punched in her agent's number. He answered on the second ring. "Zach, it's me, Paula—"

"Nice of you to think of me." His tone was unctuous. "I've been trying to reach you since last night. What happened—you forgot Stu Snyder was watching? Or you don't give a rap what he thinks?"

She closed her eyes. In point of fact, she had forgotten all about Snyder. And she was in no mood for the teasing sarcasm that was the hallmark of her agent's personality. "I'm not at home, Zach. I left last night. You were watching the broadcast, I assume?"

"Of course—"

"Belinda Raymond, the woman who was murdered, is—was my oldest and dearest friend."

There was a dubious pause. "Is that for real?"

"For real. I'm up here in Seaview. The funeral is set for late Sunday morning. I'm . . . not sure what I'll do then."

Another pause. "I'm sorry, Paula. It's life. You take the good with the bad. Do what you have to. But if you think you can do it, be back on the air Monday night."

Paula sighed. She did not respond. She could hear Zach's labored breathing.

"Aren't you going to ask," he drawled, "what Snyder thought of your broadcast?"

"No," she murmured, knowing full well he was going to tell her anyway.

He did not disappoint her. "The man's no dummy. Thinks you're class with a capital *C*."

She smiled wanly. "That's nice, Zach. Call me when he makes us an offer."

"Paula—"

"I'm sorry. I really am glad. Look, I'll call you when I get back to the city."

Hanging up, she began to pace, filled with a restless anxiety. When the phone rang, she fairly pounced on it. "Hello! . . . Hello? . . . Ted?"

The only sound was measured breathing. She slammed the receiver down hard.

CHAPTER

7

It bothered Nattlinger that the bereaved husband looked like something out of L.L. Bean—neatly dressed and clean-shaven less than twenty-four hours after finding his wife's body in a pool of blood in their kitchen.

"Sorry we have to bother you, Mr. Raymond." He offered the standard apology.

"It's all right, Officer—"

"Detective, actually. Detective Harvey Nattlinger. I'm the investigating detective assigned to follow up on Officer Garza's report."

He looked pointedly at the Cary Grant–type who stood at Raymond's side. The guy caught his drift. "Sam Pierce," he said, offering a tanned hand. "I'm a friend of Ted's—and of his wife's. Actually, Belinda worked for me."

"Mrs. Raymond worked for you?"

"Yes. She's—she was my executive administrator. I'm president of a company called Tattersall Industries. We have offices in Oakland and San Francisco, as well as here in Seaview."

Nattlinger nodded. "She work for you yesterday?"

"Yes, as a matter of fact she did. She left early—about three, I think. She was going home to get ready for her daughter's birthday party."

"So that was the last time you saw her, then. Three o'clock yesterday afternoon."

"Yes. In fact, she hadn't been gone more than twenty minutes when Ted—Mr. Raymond came by." A flash of pain crossed the Cary Grant face. "I've thought about this more than once. If he had caught her before she left, or if I hadn't detained him, she might—well, I suppose there's no point. . . ."

Nattlinger'd never heard of Tattersall Industries. He would want to talk some more to Sam Pierce. But not now. Ted Raymond, who reminded him a little of Tom Cruise, was looking decidedly edgy.

"Well, listen, Mr. Pierce"—Nattlinger's tone was curt—"I may be wantin' to get in touch with you. But right now, I need to talk to Mr. Raymond. If you like, you can have a seat out there."

He pointed to a bench on the perimeter of the squad room, which at the moment held a sleeping drunk, and left Pierce to stare at the bench while he led the way to his cubicle. Inside, he motioned Raymond to a green plastic chair and sat heavily behind his desk. When the creaks and groans of his swivel chair subsided, he looked earnestly at Raymond.

"Again, thanks for coming down here, Mr. Raymond. Hate to intrude at this time. I know you gave a statement to Officer Garza last night, so this'll be fairly routine."

Raymond nodded and Nattlinger wasn't sure if his

expression seemed to relax or if it was just the self-confidence of the naturally good-looking that was reflected in the cool, blue eyes.

"You told Officer Garza you left Mr. Pierce's office a little before four yesterday afternoon, and you stopped briefly at a party goods store on Rowan Avenue before you headed home."

Raymond seemed distracted, or annoyed, or both. "Yes. That's what I told him. Belinda—my wife—had asked me to go by and pick up a party tablecloth and napkins."

"But you didn't buy anything, you told Officer Garza, because they didn't have what you wanted."

"That's right. Belinda was very specific. It had to be Winnie the Pooh. But they didn't have it, so I figured I'd go on home and try someplace else in the morning."

Convenient, Nattlinger thought, that he couldn't find what he wanted, or he might have had a receipt with the time of purchase on it. "And you figured it must have been around four-thirty when you pulled into your driveway."

"As near as I can figure, yes, yes. Do we have to go over all this again?"

"Appreciate your patience, sir." Nattlinger worked to keep his expression bland. "We know for sure it was four-fifty-six when you dialed 911. Maybe you could just sort of go over again what happened in that intervening time."

Ted Raymond came up out of his chair with a force that nearly toppled it. "I've been through this once. I already described what I saw when I went into the kitchen. It was horrible—a nightmare. Belinda, lying there—just lying there in all that blood—and that damned kid with the knife in his hand, moaning—kind of crooning over her. . . ."

"And what did you do, sir?"

Raymond began to pace, no small feat in the tiny cubicle. "I don't remember. Knelt down and touched her. I knew she was dead. I knew she was. I knelt there and I could feel the blood—her blood—seeping into my trousers. . . . I think—I must have gone a little nuts. I started yelling at the kid, pounding him back against the kitchen cabinets, pleading with him to tell me why he did this. . . ."

Leaning back until his chair squeaked, Nattlinger rubbed the mole on his chin. The intake physical given to Danny One-Eye showed cuts and abrasions on the back of his head consistent with the bashing Raymond described. It was entirely possible Raymond was telling it just the way it happened. Was it just as possible the kid wandered in at precisely the wrong moment—and that Raymond took advantage of his natural confusion and bullied him into believing it was his fault?

Probably pushing it, Nattlinger decided as Ted Raymond sank back into his chair. He watched the guy's breathing slow to normal, then tried another tack. "You and your wife had an . . . excellent relationship, you told Officer Garza."

"Absolutely. We've been married five years. We . . . loved each other very much."

"Ever argue?"

"Of course." No hesitation. "But not very often and not for long."

Nattlinger considered. "You know this suspect, this kid who calls himself Danny One-Eye?"

"Yes, I know him. I can't tell you how many times I begged my wife not to let him come around. She let him—I don't know, do odd jobs around the house. She felt sorry for him, she said. She gave him food—money, too. I told her one day she'd regret it. . . ."

"Why was that, Mr. Raymond?"

"I don't know. He wasn't right in the head. I was afraid one day he might just . . . turn on her, maybe even hurt our daughter—like a mad dog, the proverbial mad dog who turns around and bites the hand that feeds him. . . ."

Nattlinger looked from Raymond's well-pressed pants to his earnest, open expression. Maybe it happened just the way he said. After all, the kid had confessed. "Your wife felt sorry for this Danny," he said. "She gave him food. Money. Did she ever give him anything else? Anything else you know of?"

Raymond looked wary. "No, I don't think so. Why? Why do you ask?"

He rolled back, sucked in his gut, and opened his desk drawer. He brought out an object in a clear plastic evidence bag and laid it in the middle of the desk. "Do you happen to know anything about this, Mr. Raymond? Does it look familiar at all?"

Raymond stared at the small gold earring and then looked up, frowning. "It's Belinda's. I gave them to her on our third anniversary. She told me—she told me she'd lost one. . . ."

Nattlinger spread his hands on the desk. "You're sure."

Raymond nodded.

"Our property guy found it in the suspect's pocket when they brought him in last night."

Paula tried to read, but the letters on the page might have been hieroglyphics. Besides, it was nearly five, and she was beginning to be concerned about what was taking Ted and Sam so long. Finally, she heard the front door chime and ran to open the door. It was Lissa, smiling happily, nearly hidden by a huge balloon bouquet.

"Hi, sweetie!" She put a smile on her own face. "How was your birthday party?"

"It was fun," Lissa squealed, running into the living room, where she let go of the brightly colored, helium-filled balloons and watched them float to the ceiling.

"Exhausting," Judy followed behind her, managing the giant Pooh Bear and setting down a stack of boxes, some with bits of brightly colored wrapping paper still clinging to their sides.

"I bet." Paula watched as Lissa dove headlong into the stack of presents. "But thanks, Judy. For everything. Thanks from Belinda, too."

Judy nodded. "The kids were fine. A party's a party. They were great. But some of the adults—I don't know. It was hard. Nobody knew what to say. . . ."

"I understand." Paula swallowed hard. "But I think we did the right thing. I'm no psychologist, but it seems right to me that Lissa's memories of this . . . terrible time may be tempered by pleasant memories of her party."

"Belinda made the cake, you know." There were tears in Judy's eyes. "When Ted asked me to bring Lissa home last night—after the police had gone—I offered to help, maybe scrub down the kitchen. But Ted had already done it. Well, I saw the cake, and the balloon bouquet, and that's when I thought about the party. . . ."

Paula frowned. "Ted cleaned up the kitchen?"

"Well, yes. That's what he told me."

But he'd told Paula—what was it he'd said? *They* had cleaned it up. *Somebody* . . .

Judy looked at her oddly. "Are you all right?"

"What? Oh, yes. Sorry."

"Well, anyway, Ted told me to take the cake home, along with the balloon bouquet. I'm sure it was hard for him—seeing all that party stuff in the midst of . . . all his grief."

Paula hesitated. "They were so happy, Belinda and Ted. . . ." The words seemed to slip off her tongue. "Of all the couples I know, I think they were the happiest. Didn't it seem that way to you?"

"Oh, yes!" Judy breathed. Was that the tiniest of shadows playing across her face? "They always—I mean, they seemed—well, yes, I think they were very close. . . ."

"Paula, look!" Lissa held up a pair of skates with bright orange plastic wheels. "Tiffany gave them to me. They clamp on your shoes. Can I try them? Can I take them outside?"

Paula thought about it. "Tell you what," she said finally. "You can try them out back, on the patio. Its going to be dark soon, but you can try them on the patio and then maybe on the sidewalk tomorrow."

Lissa didn't argue. She took the skates and skipped toward the sliding glass door. Paula watched her undo the lock and slip out into the dusky afternoon.

"This . . . Danny One-Eye"—she turned to Judy—"how . . . how well do you know him?"

Judy shivered. "Not well, I guess. Something about him gave me the creeps. He was always kind of . . . lurking around, as though he had nowhere to go."

"Lurking around?"

"Somehow or other, he always seemed to know when Belinda was home from the office. He would follow her around like an overgrown basset hound, waiting for her to tell him what to do."

Paula nodded. On the few occasions she'd seen him here, Belinda had treated him with respect. She had shown him the kind of simple dignity most people take for granted—but which surely must have come as a rare treat for this hulking, slow-witted youth. Perplexed, Paula looked at Judy, who must have read the question in her eyes.

"I don't know." Judy shrugged, hugging herself tightly, as if to ward off another bout of shivers. "Maybe . . . maybe he wanted more than Belinda wanted to give him."

"*Sex crime . . . The police are calling it a sex crime.*" Paula could hear Deirdre's brisk, professional voice, reporting live from the scene of "a murder only hours old. . . ."

She became aware of a car driving up, slowing, stopping in the driveway. Judy heard it, too. "I'd better be going. If there's anything else I can do . . ."

Paula reached into the pocket of her skirt. "These are the . . . arrangements for Belinda. Use your own judgment, if the neighbors want to know. . . ."

Judy took the card. "I will." She smiled shakily and touched Paula's arm. "I know you were her very best friend. She told me—well, for what it's worth, I'm going to miss her, too. . . ."

Ted's face, as he came through the doorway, was stony. He hardly seemed to see them. He pushed through the entryway without a word and headed up the stairs.

Paula turned to Sam, who shook his head slowly, his gray eyes deep and troubled.

"I'm on my way out," Judy murmured. "I'll be home if anyone needs me." She bustled through the open doorway and pulled the door closed behind her.

"A long session with the police," Sam said. "I don't know all that transpired. I do know Ted was like a caged animal by the time he was able to leave."

They moved to the living room, which was rapidly growing dim. Paula turned on the lights. Sam looked at the gaily colored balloons, the presents. "How was the party?"

"Fine," Paula told him, sinking gratefully into a cream-colored leather sofa. "I think we did the right thing, letting the party go on."

Sam nodded, sitting across from her, long legs stretched out in front of him, his fingers interlocked to form a pillow behind his head. "Ted will manage." He looked at her intently. "After all, he has you for a sounding board. But Lissa—I don't know. She may suffer the most. How does she seem to you?"

"All right at the moment." Paula was touched. "She's on the patio, trying her new skates." The sound of her screams echoed in Paula's head. "But she had terrible nightmares last night."

Sam leaned forward, and in the aura of the lamplight she could see the fine bones of his face, the way his dark hair grew in tendrils to his collar and curled carelessly around his ears.

"Maybe it's none of my business," he said. "But I have a friend. A psychologist. He specializes in working with children. I thought, maybe, if Ted . . ."

It was disconcerting, how he seemed to read her thoughts. " I planned to suggest that to Ted. Lissa will need all the help she can get. I'd be grateful if there's someone you know."

Sam had taken a business card out of a back pocket and was writing his friend's name on the back of it when they heard Ted coming down the stairs with rapid, purposeful steps.

"Here's the mate, exactly where it should have been. He had the other one all along." Ted moved toward them, holding out a hand. "Somehow, that half-wit, that Danny One-Eye, he must have managed to steal it! Probably fantasized over it, night after night, like some leering, drooling pervert!"

Paula sat, mesmerized, as Ted came closer, his open hand stretched out in front of him. In the center of his palm, glinting in the lamplight, was a small gold earring. And on his face—it was unmistakable—was a look of self-righteous triumph.

CHAPTER

—8—

Mike Shaffer tossed the Sunday funnies onto the pile of newspapers at his feet and stared morosely into the fog-shrouded woods at the far end of the arroyo.

He liked Sunday, liked the feel of it, liked to sleep a little later than usual and make himself a big breakfast. He liked to eat it out on the deck, tuned to the sounds of the arroyo, reading the paper from one end to the other while he finished a pot of coffee.

So why did this morning have a sullen edge to it, as damp and gray as the day? Why was he sitting there more out of habit than because he was enjoying any of it?

"Face it, Shaffer, you're a surly old coot." He broke off a crust of toast. "You take a perfectly nice woman like Paula Carroll and make her mad as hell at you, then you manage to muck up a perfectly good Sunday, and now you're talking to yourself." Angry, he tossed the crust over the deck in the direction of a squawking jay.

In the same split second that the jay shut up, the sun split through the fog. Mike nodded, taking it as an omen. Dammit, he was going to enjoy what was left of the quiet morning.

Determined, he carried his tray to the kitchen and set it down near the sink. Then he gathered up the remnants of his breakfast and took them out to the duck pond.

The fat, white ducks squawked and bobbed at the sight of him, rippling the surface of the pond. Kneeling on the grassy slope, he tossed them bits of bacon and toast.

When the food was gone, they squawked their disapproval and paddled away from the shore. Mike chuckled. At least they were honest about it. No pay, no play.

Rising, he went back into the house and took a fat sheaf of papers from his briefcase. He took them out back, sat down in a canvas-backed chair, and put his feet up on the edge of the deck.

For a while he convinced himself he was really concentrating, getting into the rhythm of the words. He even crossed out a phrase or two and penned a couple of notes in the margins.

But it was no use. He threw down his pencil and put the work aside. He was antsy, and there was probably nothing for it but to get himself out into the world.

Showered, he dressed in beat-up running clothes and decided he needed to exercise. But he knew, even before he left the house, where he was going to run.

It was a two-mile trek down a narrow, winding lane from the arroyo to a vee in the road, and by the time he got there, he could hear his heartbeat and feel the sweat on his back. Without breaking stride he veered right, past the closed and silent fuel tanks, toward the old downtown section the city council liked to say was "in the first stages of redevelopment."

He paused at the corner, jogging in place, waiting for the light to turn green, shaking his head at the pile of rubble that had once housed the hangouts of his youth.

He smiled, suddenly and absurdly pining for the old, rococo Strand, where you could take a date on a Saturday night and get change back from a five-dollar bill, and for Moon Burgers, too, where the after-show special got you a couple of milk shakes for a buck.

Chagrined, he wondered how much of this nostalgia was the result of his generally rotten mood, and how much was caused by his unexpected encounter yesterday with Paula Carroll.

"Ah, Shaffer"—he shook his head at the irony of it—"let's hear it for progress. Ten years ago, she didn't know you were alive. Now, she wishes you were dead."

Just past Marsden, where the street narrowed, he jogged past the old Greyhound bus depot, recently abandoned for a slick, brick building closer to the new shopping mall. He had heard somewhere that the old depot had become a haven for derelicts—that the cops tended to look the other way as long as there was no trouble. Turning the corner, he jogged around to the back of the building and yanked open a scarred metal door.

Inside the old depot, daylight filtered through the high windows in great, dusty shafts and fell, like trapezoidal spotlights, on sections of the torn and pitted floor. But the corners of the cavernous room were dark and Mike moved toward them cautiously, the only sound the soft plath-plath of his running shoes on the tile.

Eyes adjusting to the half-light, he began to make sense out of the eerie shapes—a blanket strung between two sawhorses here, and over there the misshapen, empty carcass of a Maytag washing machine carton.

"Anybody home?" His voice sounded hollow in the great, empty room. "I'm not a cop. I might have a few bucks for somebody with some information."

He listened, but he heard nothing. He peered into the empty carton. There was an old army blanket and a stack of newspapers in it and a vaguely sour smell, but if someone inhabited the box by night, there was no one in it now.

"Yo!" he hollered, moving stealthily toward what looked like a pile of rags. It was then that he saw the wary eyes staring from an inert form.

The man—at least he thought it was a man—did not move a muscle, just peered at Mike through half-lidded eyes with a vaguely menacing expression.

Mike moved a step closer, wondering how many homeless there could possibly be in a town the size of Seaview. "Yo," he said again, keeping his hands in plain view so the guy could see they were empty. "Look, man, I don't want anything from you except some information about a friend. Guy name of Danny One-Eye. I thought maybe you might know him."

The man stared in such unblinking silence that Mike began to wonder if he were dead. Hearing the man's heart beat, Mike moved a little nearer, then jumped at the sudden sound.

"Close enough, man." The voice was rough, a deep, drawling baritone. "I can see you ain' no cop. What you wannin' here?"

He cleared his throat. "I was asking about Danny One-Eye."

"What you want wi' Danny One-Eye?"

Mike blinked, not believing his luck. "You know Danny?"

A pause. "Maybe."

"Yeah, well, you haven't seen him around for a couple of days, have you? That's because he's locked up in the city jail. I happen to be his lawyer."

"Jail beats dead." The man closed his eyes, his grudging curiosity satisfied.

By now Mike could make out a thin, rumpled form, an elongated face, a thatch of beard. "Listen," he said, "I'd like to help Danny, but I don't know much about him. Five bucks if you know any more than I do. Ten if you can show me where he crashes."

One eye opened. "Show me the ten."

Mike reached into a back pocket, hauled out his wallet, and was relieved to see he had two tens and a five. He held out a ten and let it flutter to the ground, as if to prove to the guy that he trusted him.

A scrawny arm darted out for the bill, a thumb jerked to one side.

"That's where he crashes?" Mike was already moving in the direction of the cursory thumb-jerk.

"Yeah, man, but there ain' nothin' there."

Mike stopped in his tracks. "Right. Right, I can see that. You, uh, wouldn't happen to know where his stuff is, would you?"

"Nope."

"No, of course not."

"Man disappears for two, three days, guys figure he ain' comin' back."

"Right, I can dig that." Mike turned back, already reaching for his wallet. "There's another ten if you happen to know where any of his stuff might have gone."

The eyes opened, locked on the ten, deliberated only briefly. Then the scrawny arm reached into the shadows, came up with a squarish, boxlike object, and tossed it in Mike's direction.

Mike's hand shot out by instinct, and his fingers closed around the cold, metal object, which on closer inspection was a red plaid tin that once had held imported English cookies. "This it?"

The man shrugged. "All I know 'bout, man. Some other dude musta snagged his blanket."

Mike nodded, handing over the ten. "Why does he call himself Danny One-Eye?"

A shrug from the shadows.

He tried again. "Do you want to know why he's in jail?"

No answer.

"They say he murdered a woman. What do you think about that?"

He waited, but he knew it was a lost cause. The man was feigning sleep. Hefting the cookie tin, he turned on his heel. "Well. It was nice doing business with you."

He was halfway to the door when the voice rumbled toward him. "No lie. Y'all have a nice day."

On Sunday evening Paula opened the car window a crack to let in the damp coastal air. It had been a long day, and she longed for nothing more than her own familiar bed. If traffic stayed light, she'd be home in half an hour, but she knew she would have to fight to stay alert.

She'd awakened that morning from a restless sleep feeling as though she'd been drugged. Her first conscious thought was that this was the day they were going to bury Belinda. Her second—and this she'd noted with relief—was that Lissa had slept through the night.

Turning to read the bedside clock, she'd been surprised to see it was nearly seven. Her eyes felt gritty and her throat dry, as though she hadn't had enough sleep despite the fact that she'd gone to bed a little more than eight hours earlier.

With effort, she'd flung the covers aside and shivered in the morning cool. Then, tying on an old chenille robe, she'd padded down the hall to Lissa's room.

The door had been left just slightly ajar, in case the child woke again during the night. Peering inside, she could see Lissa lying there, hear her even breathing.

Shivering again, she pulled her robe tighter and headed down the stairs. It was quiet and she assumed that Ted, too, had managed to sleep in a bit. But when she reached the kitchen, she found a note propped up against the toaster: "*Couldn't sleep. Went out for a drive. Back before long. Ted.*"

She'd made coffee and watched mindlessly as it dripped into the pot, trying hard to block out everything except getting them all through the day.

Ted had been ambivalent the night before when Paula suggested that Lissa be allowed to attend the memorial service, and Sam, bless his tactful heart, had not presumed to take sides. But they *had* put in a call to Sam's friend, a Dr. James Irvin, who said that as long as the casket was closed and there would be no viewing of the body, the child might benefit from the opportunity to say a final good-bye to her mother.

In the end, Ted had relented—and he also agreed that Lissa would probably do well to have a few sessions with Dr. Irvin.

Now, as she drove toward San Francisco, Paula opened the car window a little wider and breathed in the salt-tinged air. It had been hard to leave Lissa—so very hard, though Paula planned to go back to Seaview the next weekend. Till then, she'd taken comfort from Judy Morrissey's promise to keep a close eye on the child.

The chapel service had been brief and tasteful—with mercifully little intrusion by the press. And when they returned to the house on Rutledge Avenue, they found the neighbors had prepared a repast.

"Mommy's okay now," Lissa had told Paula soberly when she'd taken her upstairs at bedtime. "Something had happened to her, but she's all better now, even though she had to go away."

Paula'd looked at her, grateful but surprised that she seemed to understand so well. "That's exactly right," she told her softly. "And she will always—"

"Always love me. You told me that, Paula. And so did Sam. He told me the same thing."

Paula smiled, enormously grateful for Sam's tranquil presence.

Ted had been quiet, almost distant all day, after coming home from his early morning drive. She supposed it was just his way of coping with the emotional toll of it all, but it was comforting to know that Sam would be close by if Ted—or Lissa—should need him.

She'd hugged Lissa tightly, then cupped her cheek gently as she tucked her into bed. "Listen," she told her, "I have to go home tonight because I have to go to work. I'll be back next weekend, but until then, you and Sam will have to take extra good care of Daddy—and each other."

"We will," Lissa promised, her eyes fluttering as she nestled into her pillow.

Paula'd wanted to tell her that she would telephone often—every day until she got back. But the long lashes curving over the rosy cheek told her Lissa had already drifted off.

Now Paula sighed, feeling suddenly bereft—and more than a little helpless. She wondered if Ted would be ready by next weekend to make some serious decisions.

The lights of San Francisco came steadily closer, amorphous shapes becoming familiar landmarks and finally the streetlamps of her neighborhood. Paula stretched to make herself stay alert until she pulled into her own driveway.

Turning off the engine, she slumped against the wheel, wearier than she could ever remember being. Forcing herself to move, she reached for her overnight bag and slung it over her shoulder. Then she grabbed her purse and tucked it under her arm as she fumbled for her door key.

She thought briefly about stopping for her mail, but it didn't seem worth the effort. Glad to be home, she turned her key in the lock and moved into the darkened living room.

It was then that the memory sprang to her consciousness—the elusive thought that had been teasing her: the phone call! The phone call she'd gotten when she'd come home from the studio the other night. In her shock, in the midst of her raw grief, she had somehow managed to bury it. But now it surfaced, and she shivered in the cold.

Who had warned her away from Seaview—and why?

CHAPTER

—9—

Mike Shaffer dressed quickly on Monday, fumbling with the knot of his tie. Danny One-Eye's arraignment was set for 2:00 P.M., and he had a lot to do before then.

He'd jogged all the way home yesterday holding the red plaid tin he'd paid the transient twenty bucks for, but he'd waited until he'd showered and changed before he finally pried it open—and he wouldn't have been a bit surprised to find nothing in it of Danny's.

Except for a harmonica with abalone shell trim, what he'd rummaged through was a motley collection of junk: old matchbooks, a handkerchief, some mangy spools of thread—the kinds of things any transient might have found and stowed away for who knew what reason. But near the bottom were two items that seemed to link the possessions to its owner: a plastic nametag that read *White Rock Academy*—and a snapshot of Belinda Raymond.

White Rock Academy was something of a misnomer. Mike recognized the name immediately. It was a county facility some forty miles down the coast that housed juvenile wards of the court.

Armed with the box, he'd gone down to the jail and asked to see his client, who identified it as his, pawed through it and immediately plucked out the harmonica.

"Do you play the harmonica?" Mike asked.

Danny nodded and put it to his lips. But then he caught sight of the snapshot of Belinda, and he cried out her name and began to bawl.

"Where did you get this snapshot, Danny?"

Sobbing. "From her . . . from Belinda. . . ."

"From Belinda. Belinda gave you the snapshot?"

"Uh-huh. . . . She said . . . I could have it."

Mike tried to keep him talking. "You liked Belinda, didn't you, Danny?"

Danny blubbered. "I like her. But I hurt her."

"Why would you hurt Belinda if you liked her?"

The boy-man's face was a mask of agony. "I twist the knife. I kill her."

Mike tried every way he knew how to get his client to open up, to tell his story from beginning to end in a calm and logical way. But Danny was anything but calm and logical. He floundered in his own private hell, and words, when he reached for them, often failed him.

In the end, there were only two things that Mike Shaffer knew for sure: one, that his client, whoever he was, was convinced he'd killed Belinda Raymond—and two, that if he were made to take the stand, he would do nothing to help his own cause.

Knotting his tie for the third time, Mike glanced at his bedroom clock. Eight-ten. It was an hour's drive to White Rock Academy, and the director was supposed to be there by nine-thirty. With luck, Mike would talk to him, find out what he could and get back in plenty of time for the arraignment.

Paula slept badly despite a long, hot bath and a glass of warm milk laced with brandy. She was up before sunrise, annoyed with herself since she didn't need to be at the studio until noon—and aware that Rollie would have a makeup man's fit over the dark circles under her eyes.

While the coffee brewed, she dipped cotton pads in warm witch hazel and dabbed at the under-eye puffiness, but she gave up when it became clear that the home remedy was useless and settled for a palmful of expensive moisturizer and the hope of an afternoon nap.

Pouring a mugful of strong coffee, she settled herself on the sofa and pulled a heavy, handmade blue and white afghan up around her terry-clad shoulders. She'd spent hours sleeping fitfully, trying to recall the timbre of the voice on the telephone— the harsh whisper Friday night exhorting her to "stay away from Seaview." But whoever it was had done a good job of disguising a normal voice. No matter how she tried, she couldn't seem to dredge up even a glimmer of recognition.

Not that it mattered. She *had* gone to Seaview and she would go again, of course, as long as Lissa and Ted needed her. Somehow, together, they had managed to weather the awful reality of Belinda's death, and somehow, together, they would help one another rebuild their shattered lives.

Extricating her right arm from the warm cocoon of the afghan, she rummaged around in the bookcase beside her and pulled out a leather-bound volume.

UC Santa Cruz, 1987. She traced the gold letters with a finger, then set the book down squarely on her lap and opened it to the junior class pages.

She found her own picture first, and she had to smile at the sight of her "big hair," a longish mass whorling and looping in tawny hanks around her sweatered shoulders.

Someone had once made the bitter mistake of calling her "the Barbara Walters of campus TV," but Paula had set him straight with the stinging assertion that she had better hair, better teeth, and infinitely better diction.

She smiled again, mollified to the extent that she had tried her best to use them to her advantage, and it seemed—if Zach were anywhere near right—that some network brass might at last agree.

Turning the slick, heavy pages to the T's, she found Belinda's face: pretty, dark eyes in an oval face framed by a fall of silky hair, a hint of mischief shining through the serious, pensive demeanor. *Belinda Talmadge,* the caption read, *legal eagle and a friend to the end.*

Brushing away tears, Paula flipped through the pages until she came to the photo she was looking for: she and Belinda, in hillbilly costumes, heads together onstage, singing their hearts out in a loud duet that was the smash of the Junior Class Talent Show.

Mugging and drawling, they brought the house down—and no one but Paula ever knew how scared stiff Belinda had been at the very thought of performing. A pre-law major, Belinda'd only agreed to be in the show because Paula had begged and cajoled. If the truth were known, Belinda was happiest in the quiet recesses of the library—or at least she *was* until a certain blue-eyed senior managed to get her attention.

Paula flipped through pages again until she found photos of the winter formal, Belinda radiant in white tulle, dancing with Ted Raymond. Gosh, he was handsome, even then. Paula had staked him out herself—and she had to admit she'd been more than a little surprised when he'd passed up her outrageous flirting in favor of the quiet Belinda.

Paula smiled. But she'd been happy, too. She could have had her pick of any other guy on campus, and Belinda had bloomed—positively bloomed—under Ted's singular attentiveness.

"*We talk about everything,*" she'd told Paula breathlessly. "*He wants to know what I think. It's like—I'm the most important thing in his life. He really cares what I think. . . .*"

And he did, everyone knew it. It wasn't just talk. Ted clearly adored Belinda. Even Paula, who was happily flitting from flower to flower, could recognize love when she saw it, and she saw it not just in the eyes of her friend but in the eyes of the dashing Ted Raymond.

In the spring of that year, just before he graduated, Ted asked Belinda to marry him—and she promised she would, the following spring, just as soon as she got her degree. It meant the end of Belinda's plans for law school. Ted had taken his job with the state, but he was stationed in San Diego—and the distance between them was almost more than the two of them could bear. Belinda managed to get through her senior year—but only because her wedding loomed at the end of it.

And then . . . and then . . . Paula sighed, remembering as though it were yesterday. . . .

"What's the first thing you're going to do after graduation?"

"Burn all my books in a bonfire."

"Oh, Paula, be serious for once. What's the first thing you're going to do?"

"I don't know, Belinda. Look for a job, I guess. And we all know what you're going to do."

Belinda could hardly miss the irritation in her voice. "Oh, Paula, I thought you were happy for me."

"I am happy. You know I am." Paula'd lightened her tone. "I couldn't love you more if we were sisters. Come on, Belinda, you tell me. What's the very first thing you're going to do?"

Belinda smiled. "Get our marriage license, while Ted's still up here for graduation. I'm going home next weekend, did I tell you? To get my blood test and stuff. We'll take care of that, and then Ted can go back and work for another month until the wedding. . . ."

Watching Belinda's animated face, Paula had been ashamed of her selfishness. How could she, even for one minute, cast a shadow over her best friend's happiness?

Someone had written "Sweethearts of Santa Cruz" under the winter formal photo of Belinda and Ted. Paula looked at the photo again, then gently closed the yearbook. She reached for her coffee, but it had grown stone cold. Disentangling herself from the afghan, she went to pour a second cup before she showered and shampooed her hair.

She wanted to believe they'd remained sweethearts—the sweethearts of Santa Cruz forever. And in her heart, she did believe it, despite the fact that Belinda had told her there was a problem she needed to talk about.

Surely the problem was only temporary—the kind of thing that comes up in every marriage. Whatever it was, it would surely have been resolved, if Belinda—if Belinda had lived.

But Belinda was dead. A sex crime, they called it. And Danny One-Eye was in jail—for murdering a woman who had never shown him anything but loving kindness.

Paula shivered. Damn Mike Shaffer and his insinuations about Ted. The half-wit, Danny, would be convicted and spend the rest of his wretched life behind bars. It would not bring Belinda back to them, but it might make them feel a little safer.

The coffee tasted bitter. Paula poured it down the drain, walked into the bathroom, and ran the water hot.

She dressed carefully in an emerald-green suit that brought out the color of her eyes. Rollie would be pleased. The warm witch hazel had helped a little, after all, and Paula began to feel she was back in control—at least in the world she knew best.

She was full of self-confidence when she slipped on her shoes and went out to get her mail. Perhaps that was why it rattled her so—literally took her breath away—to find the door of her mailbox torn off its hinges, exposing the envelopes inside.

She grew angry, furious. More than that, she felt *violated,* as though it were *she* who was lying there, naked and vulnerable and exposed to the elements, milky white against a dark, gaping hole.

Her breath came in great, ragged gasps. Who would do such a thing? A vandal? Not likely, since none of the boxes on either side of hers had been even slightly disturbed.

Slowly, she reached into the opened box and

retrieved the mail inside. A thief? Why? What could a thief have possibly hoped to steal? Nobody sent cash in the mail anymore—certainly not to her.

Working hard to marshal her senses, Paula took the mail inside, spread the envelopes on the breakfast bar near the telephone and tried to figure out what might have been taken—and by whom.

Of course, it was impossible, searching for something when she had no clue what it was, but it helped to have something to focus on until she felt her anger subside. She would have to report it to management immediately and demand to have the box fixed right away.

She was halfway to the studio before the notion struck that it might have something to do with Belinda—something Belinda had sent her, perhaps a letter that someone wanted to intercept. . . .

It seemed preposterous—but wasn't it also preposterous that someone had threatened Paula on the telephone? And wasn't it preposterous that Belinda was dead and that nobody knew for sure who had killed her?

Two things Paula knew for certain, and she drew no comfort from either: Whoever it was, it was not Danny One-Eye who'd made that phone call the night Belinda was murdered . . . and it was not Danny One-Eye—who was in the Seaview jail—who had ripped her mailbox apart. . . .

CHAPTER

—►10◄—

The interim director of White Rock Academy was a man named Otis Tremont, a balding black man with a ready smile and a firm, dry handshake.

"'Fraid I can't help much," he told Mike Shaffer, studying the small police photo. "Without a name, I can't check the files. I doubt we had him here as Danny One-Eye."

"I understand that." Mike was impatient. "I was hoping maybe someone on your staff has been around here long enough to recognize the guy and possibly supply us with a name."

Tremont shrugged and picked up the phone. "Rennie, how long you been here at White Rock? . . . Uh-huh. Happen to know anybody on staff been here longer than that—not a counselor, necessarily—just anybody on the grounds?"

Mike fidgeted, looking at his watch.

"Uh-huh," Tremont was saying. "Well, why don't you see if you can round him up. Tell him I need to see him right away."

Mike glanced around the cream-colored office, with its scarred, standard, county-issue furniture, and sat still for small talk about the mild January weather until an older black man poked his grizzled head into the doorway.

"Eh, Otis, you wantin' to see me?"

Tremont motioned the old man in. "George, this is Mike Shaffer. He's a public defender up in Seaview, trying to get an ID on a guy. Mr. Shaffer, this is George Tulley. He's a gardener—been here twenty years."

"Nice to meet you, Mr. Tulley." Mike handed over the snapshot. "I was hoping maybe you'd recognize this man—help me get a line on who he is."

Tulley looked at the grainy snapshot and grinned, exposing large, yellowed teeth. "Man, that's Danny One-Eye! Know 'im anyplace. He was here since he was a boy."

Mike cleared his throat. "Uh, Danny One-Eye. That isn't his real name, is it, sir?"

"Naw, naw." Tulley shook his head. "That's what everbuddy called 'im. Hey, now." He cast a wary glance at Mike. "Is Danny in some kind of trouble?"

"Could be, Mr. Tulley." Mike opted for the truth. "The police think he murdered a woman."

"Murder? Danny?" Tulley looked incredulous. "Ol' Danny, he couldn't hurt no one. Couldn't even stand it to see people fight. That's how come he got his name."

"One-Eye?"

"Yeah." Tulley chuckled. "Danny, he was somethin' else. Boys here, you know, they all the time fightin', heaven only know what for. But Danny, hell, from the time he was a tyke, he'd cry ever' time he saw a fight—just hunker on down and cover up 'is eyes.

'Cept he always *peeked* a little outta one eye, you know—like somethin' in him jist had to know if anyone was gettin' bad hurt."

Mike nodded. "Peeked out of one eye. So the kids called him Danny One-Eye."

"Yeah," Tulley grinned again. "Name just stuck after a while."

"What about his real name? The name he came in with. Do you think you could bring it to mind?"

Tulley thought, narrowing his eyes. "Name was somethin' . . . somethin' like a *gentleman*. . . ." The old man smiled and the sun broke through. "Gentry! That's his name! Danny Gentry!"

Mike turned to Tremont, who needed no instruction to get on the phone to his secretary. He looked back at Tulley. "You're a gem, Mr. Tulley. Gentry. Do you remember when he left here?"

Tulley thought. "Three, four year ago. Musta been sixteen or seventeen. Some uncle showed up, had a farm or something in Mendocino. Ol' Danny, he went to live with him."

George Tulley's memory was pretty darned perfect, according to the chart Tremont handed Mike.

Danny Gentry had been a ward of the court since he was four, when he was found, abandoned by persons unknown, in a public parking lot on the outskirts of Seaview. Lacking good verbal skills, he had been unable to tell the authorities much of anything besides his name. When routine investigations failed to turn up any relatives, he had been housed at White Rock Academy, where he'd remained until four years ago, when he was approximately sixteen and an uncle showed up, seemingly out of nowhere.

Mike handed the file to Tremont. "Can you run me

a copy of this? I'm going to want his IQ test scores as well as his history at White Rock." He turned to Tulley. "You liked Danny, didn't you?"

The old man grinned. "Yeah, I liked him. Me and Danny, we was buddies. He used to help me sometimes, out on the grounds—trimmin' bushes, spreadin' fertilizer. He could learn how to do stuff like that, you know—stuff that didn't take no book learnin'. Good with flowers, too, know what I mean? . . . Murder! No way, not Danny One-Eye. That kid wouldn't swat a fly on his nose. Kid's got the soul of a creampuff."

Mike smiled. "If it came to that, would you say those things in court? Tell a judge how you remember Danny—just the way you told me?"

Tulley worked his lower jaw. "Don't much care about courts. Still, if it came to it, I reckon I would. Ain't nuthin' but the truth. . . ."

In some ways it seemed to Paula that she'd been away for weeks. So much had happened since Friday night that the studio had a surreal quality. She was glad she had walked out after the Friday broadcast without a word to anyone. She couldn't have taken it if she'd had to sit there and receive condolences from her colleagues.

But she couldn't fool Rollie, who looked at her morosely.

"It appears we've had a bit of a Weekend."

She smiled, hearing the capital W. "Yes, I guess you could say that."

A wicked smile. "Well, sweetface, I certainly hope it was worth it. You come see Rollie half an hour early. This may take heroic measures."

Paula laughed, picking up her script and heading toward her dressing room. Betty Lou had said it was a slow news day, so there shouldn't be any surprises. Paula could simply get familiar with the script and prepare to sparkle on the air.

She was halfway through the script when somebody knocked. "Paula? It's me—Deirdre."

"Deirdre, come in!"

The reporter smiled at her from the doorway. "Do you have a minute?"

"Sure!"

Deirdre nodded and stepped into the room, carrying a small sheaf of papers. "This is weird, Paula, another story out of Seaview. Isn't that where your home is?"

Paula tensed. "Yes. I was born there—lived there till I went away to college."

Deirdre nodded. "Well, you may remember I covered a murder there the other night."

Paula nodded, her throat dry.

"Well, now there's this other thing. No tie-in, I'm sure, but I thought, since Seaview's your hometown, maybe you can help me get a handle on it."

Paula felt herself relax a little. She motioned Deirdre to a seat on the sofa. "Sure I'll help, if I can."

"As you probably know, there's an old oil refinery up there." Deirdre sat and put on her glasses.

"There was. My father used to work there. But I think it's been closed down."

"It has." Deirdre nodded, looking at her notes. "Apparently it was being used as a fuel storage and blending facility—until it started leaking hazardous waste. There are piles of PCB-laced soil all around it and maybe contaminated groundwater. A real health hazard, according to officials, not to mention an environmental nightmare."

Paula frowned. "I had no idea—"

"Neither did anybody else—till the state Department of Public Health stepped in and declared it a public danger. Along with everything else, there's a danger of explosions if the excess gases aren't maintained."

Paula nodded. "So what's the problem now that the state has stepped in? Won't they clean it up?"

Deirdre shrugged. "That's the heart of it. It's a forty million dollar cleanup. The state wants the company who owns it to clean it up, but it seems the company's in bankruptcy. The owners filed a motion to abandon the site and got a court order allowing them to do it—so now it's unclear who's responsible and who's on the financial hook."

Paula blinked. "And meanwhile, the public danger goes on. The site could be a time bomb ticking. . . ." *Contaminated groundwater.* She thought of Lissa. Her school was less than a mile away from there.

"You got it." Deirdre gestured. "That's the nature of my story. The hazard nobody's owning up to. I was hoping, since you know the area, you might know something about the owner."

Paula cocked her head. "Who is it?"

"The company's in Las Vegas. Duncan Associates. The president is a Wynn Davidson."

"Las Vegas? Nevada?"

Deirdre looked at her notes. "That's what our sources say."

Paula shook her head. "When my father worked there, it was owned by Foster Oil. But that was years ago, when it was a major refinery. It could have been sold any number of times since then. I'm sorry, Deirdre. I wish I could help, but I've never heard of Wynn Davidson—or Duncan Associates."

Deirdre sighed. "Oh, well, thanks anyway. I

thought it was worth a try. I just can't seem to get to these guys. They've filed bankruptcy, their offices are closed—no matter what direction I go in, there seems to be nobody home."

The younger reporter got up to go, gathered her papers together. "By the way, Paula—Seaview's not all that big—did you happen to know that woman who was killed there? The one I reported on Friday?"

"Yes, Deirdre, I knew her." Paula kept her voice even. "I knew her. I—went to school with her."

"Oh, my gosh." Deirdre's eyes were wide. "Really? Oh, how awful! But at least they've got the guy who did it. I hope they nail him to the wall."

The voice seemed to echo in the silence long after Deirdre had gone: *At least they've got the guy who did it. I hope they nail him to the wall. . . ."*

But *did* they have the guy who did it? Or was it someone else? Someone who didn't want Paula to learn what had been bothering Belinda . . . someone who'd go to extraordinary lengths to keep her from finding out . . . ?

Ted's face swam into her consciousness, and she fought to push it away. Damn you, Mike Shaffer, what possible reason— No! There was no way!

All at once Paula felt suffocated in the small, crowded dressing room. She tossed aside her script and got up to go, but she stepped on something soft. She bent to pick it up. Deirdre's eyeglass case. It must have slipped off her lap. Well, she would find her, return the case, then spend some more time with the script.

She turned the case over and over in her hands. She thought about what Deirdre had told her. As if there weren't enough to worry about, now there was a hazardous refinery site—not four miles from the Raymond house, not far from Lissa's school. . . .

Duncan Associates. She was sure she'd never heard of them. Why would she, if they were located in Las Vegas? For that matter, she'd been away from Seaview so long she might not know them even if they were local.

Paula sighed, on the verge of tears. Suddenly it was all too much. She felt like a dinghy cast adrift on a strange and silent sea. Alone! That was it. For the first time in her life, she was completely and totally alone. There was no one she could talk to, no one to trust. *Oh, Belinda, how I miss you!*

The telephone rang, startling her so that the eyeglass case slipped from her fingers. In a fluid motion she bent to retrieve it, then picked up the phone. She took a deep breath. "Paula Carroll."

"Paula!" The voice was resonant. "Gosh, I never thought I'd actually get through! This is Sam. Sam Pierce."

CHAPTER

— 11 —

It began to sprinkle five miles out of Seaview, and by the time Mike reached the county courthouse, it had turned into a purposeful downpour.

It was ten minutes of two, and parking would be tight—plus he had no umbrella in the car. Muttering to himself, Mike pulled into the lot and made two fruitless passes around the courthouse. On the third pass, as he considered taking his chances in a spot reserved for judges, a black Celica pulled out, missing his front bumper by inches, and Mike pulled in and cut the engine of his gray Ford Tempo.

Holding an old newspaper over his head, he grabbed up his briefcase and made a run for the courthouse, aware that his socks and the cuffs of his trousers were getting thoroughly soaked. By the time he reached Department Six, he felt like yesterday's laundry and rivulets of water were dripping from his hair and sliding under his collar.

It did not improve his mood to see Harvey Natt-linger sitting in the back of the courtroom, two hundred and twenty pounds of somber cop with a bulging shirtfront and an attitude. It was customary for the investigating officer to be present for an arraignment in a murder case, but Mike had the feeling that Nattlinger's interest was more than cursory. Mopping the back of his neck with a Kleenex, he nodded a greeting toward the beefy cop as he proceeded toward the front of the courtroom.

Danny was seated at the defense table, dressed in an orange jail jumpsuit and looking more puzzled than frightened. Mike had spent an hour yesterday telling Danny what to expect, that a judge would read the charges against him and ask whether he was guilty or not guilty.

That had been the hardest part, trying to make Danny understand that he was entitled to tell his story—to have a jury of his peers decide whether Danny understood what had happened on the day of Belinda Raymond's death and what his part in her death had been.

He was sliding into a chair next to his client when the clerk called the court to order, and he reached over and gently pulled Danny to his feet as Judge Dina Marquez approached the bench.

She was a tall woman with a regal bearing and a no-nonsense expression who had started out as an assistant district attorney and come up through the ranks. While it was well known that she wouldn't stand for fancy courtroom shenanigans, she had a reputation for infinite patience and careful deliberation. Mike thought Danny could do worse than to draw her courtroom for his trial—if it came to trial, he reminded himself, with an apprehensive glance at his client.

As it turned out, he need not have worried about

Danny's blurting out a guilty plea. When the judge addressed him, the color drained from Danny's face, and he looked over, panicked, at Mike.

"My client enters a plea of not guilty, your honor," Mike said firmly.

Judge Marquez glanced at Danny and then looked squarely at Mike. "I have read and considered the police report and all pertinent documents and, based on the information at hand and the plea you have entered on his behalf, I must order your client— Danny One-Eye—bound over for trial."

Mike nodded, and Judge Marquez went on without missing a beat. "I am also, based upon your client's alleged diminished mental capacity, ordering that he be examined by a forensic psychologist to determine his understanding of these proceedings."

It was standard procedure in cases like this for a court-appointed psychologist to get involved, in order to determine whether the suspect knew right from wrong and the condition of his mental state— not only at the time of the alleged offense but afterward and at the present time.

"Yes, your honor." Mike nodded again, knowing that he would have requested the examination if the judge had not ordered it on her own.

A date was set three weeks hence to receive the psychologist's report, and Judge Marquez rose from the bench and solemnly left the courtroom.

Mike turned to Danny amid a flurry of activity as reporters and courtroom junkies milled about. "You did fine, Danny," he told him. "Everything's okay. You're going to get to tell your story."

Danny blinked. "Belinda's dead. Danny killed Belinda."

• • •

Paula rarely went out to dinner before her 10:00 P.M. broadcast, but she had to admit it felt good tonight, and she looked at Sam Pierce with amusement.

"What's funny?" he asked, with that incredible way he had of seeming to read her mind.

"Not actually funny," she told him, swirling the wine in her glass. "It's just that your timing was so impeccable. I was—licking my wounds when you called."

"Licking your wounds?"

Paula nodded. "Feeling sorry for myself. It was as though it hit me all at once. Belinda's—really gone."

Sam looked at her. "She was your closest friend."

"More than that. She was—an extension of me. Oh, it's hard to explain: We've been friends since childhood, and neither of us had any siblings. I guess we long ago passed friendship. There was a bond between us. We were like sisters."

"What about family?"

"There isn't much. My mother died when I was ten. My father raised me, but he died six years ago—three months after he retired."

Sam poured more wine. "I'm so sorry. And Belinda's parents are gone, too. I remember they were killed in an auto accident shortly after Belinda came to work for me."

Paula sighed. "It was like losing my mother twice. We've . . . been through a lot together, Belinda and I."

"And Ted. . . ."

Paula looked up sharply. "And Ted. Yes, of course. Ted, too. . . ."

There was silence for a moment, and then a shy

smile eased into Sam's expression. "You know, she always wanted us to get together. Belinda—did she ever tell you?"

Paula had to laugh. "At least ten times. Something always got in the way. You were out of town, or I was busy—but, yes, I know she wanted us to meet."

His expression grew serious, his gray eyes soft. "I can't tell you how sad I am that it had to be—under these circumstances. But at the same time I have to say that I'm awfully glad we finally have met."

Paula swallowed over a lump in her throat. "Well, tell me something about yourself, Sam Pierce. I know you are a wildly successful businessman."

He chuckled. "I don't know about wildly successful. I've been a little lucky, I guess. I inherited Tattersall Industries from my father and I've managed to—well, diversify us a little."

"Diversify. What a lovely word." Paula pushed her plate away. "What, exactly, is Tattersall Industries? What have you diversified from?"

"Originally it was lumber. My father had been a rancher. He put great stock in the land. But then he branched out into shipping and construction, maybe a little too quickly. Things were a little shaky when I took over the companies but, as I said, I've been lucky. I've managed to get us into enough areas to keep us generally solvent."

Paula was impressed, though she suspected his success had more to do with drive than with luck. "Belinda told me you have offices in San Francisco as well as Seaview—and heaven knows where else."

"Denver. Chicago. I'm thinking about New York, but I'm not sure I'm that sophisticated."

She had to laugh. "Not that sophisticated! What are you doing in Seaview? I should think it must seem a little small-town next to all your other venues."

He shrugged. "I like it. It's a good place to live. It helps me keep things in perspective. I was born in Salinas—I'm a country boy at heart. And, anyway, Seaview is growing."

Paula nodded. "So it is. I'm not sure I like where it's going. When they tear down grand old movie houses like the Strand and replace them with little concrete boxes . . ."

Sam's expression turned decidedly sheepish.

"Oh, no," Paula said. "Yours?"

He held up his hands, "Guilty. Sorry. But the old Strand had been condemned. I remember when Ted did the site inspection for the state and—"

"Yes, yes, I know."

He smiled at Paula, the skin crinkling around his deepset gray eyes. "For you, I will ask the city council for a variance. I will build a bigger and better Strand."

Paula laughed. "No, no. For you, I will learn to like little cement boxes."

He started to pour more wine, but Paula covered her glass. "Not for me. I still have a show to do."

"Of course. And I promised to get you back by eight." He motioned to the waiter for the check.

Paula considered. "I do have a question. Since you're in business in Seaview, maybe you can help."

"Ask away," he said, reaching for his wallet.

"Do you know of a company named Duncan Associates? Or a man by the name of Wynn Davidson? Duncan is apparently a Nevada company, but they own what's left of the old refinery in Seaview."

"Duncan Associates. Davidson. I don't think I know them. I thought the refinery was Foster Oil's."

Paula nodded. "It was, years ago. My father used to work for Foster. Apparently, it's been sold to these Duncan people—and there's some question about fiscal responsibility." She paused. "Did you know the Department of Public Health has declared the site a public danger?"

Sam grimaced. "I'd heard something about it. Wasn't sure how serious it was."

"Well, it's very serious. PCB in the soil. Gas leaks. Contaminated groundwater."

He looked up. "Are you sure?"

"That's what the state says."

"Then why aren't they cleaning it up?"

"Good question." Paula brushed crumbs from her skirt. "The state's trying to get the owners to foot the bill—and the owners are playing footsy, trying to wriggle out of it. I guess they've declared bankruptcy."

Sam signed the check and looked at his watch. "We'll make it back by eight if we walk fast."

"We'd better be back by eight, or there'll be hell to pay. My makeup man's a force to reckon with."

Sam smiled, taking her easily by the arm and guiding her out of the restaurant. "Well, I wish I could be more helpful," he told her. "This is more than a fiscal problem. I live in Seaview. I don't like the idea of—what did you say? Contaminated groundwater?"

Paula was fairly tall, but she had to lengthen her stride to keep up with Sam's pace. "And the possibility of explosions. It's more than a little scary. Lissa's school is very near the refinery site."

There were puddles in the street from the afternoon's rain. Reflections from the streetlamps shimmered wetly. Sam took her arm again as they crossed the street and slowed in front of her building.

"Well, I'll certainly put my ear to the wall," he said. "See what I can find out. If I do hear anything, I'll let you know. I take it you're doing a story."

"We are, yes. I just found out about it today. And, of course, we have a vested interest."

"So we do." His eyes met hers, and she felt the most delicious shiver. "Paula, I can't tell you how glad I am that I reached you this afternoon."

"Me, too. You've been a tonic. How much longer will you be in San Francisco?"

"Just until tomorrow morning, I'm afraid. Then I have to be back in Seaview. When are you going back?"

"This weekend."

"Good. Will I see you then?"

Paula nodded. "Yes."

There was an awkward silence.

"Watch my broadcast tonight."

"Count on it. I'm on my way to the hotel."

She looked into his eyes.

"You're very beautiful."

She felt herself shiver again.

CHAPTER

~12~

There were two huge bouquets of flowers in her dressing room on Tuesday.

One was from Zach, with a note saying Stu Snyder was definitely interested and that they would call to set up a lunch or dinner date with her later in the week.

The other was from Sam. The card read, *"You're the top. See you this weekend."*

Paula smiled, still astonished that Sam had called her yesterday afternoon when she'd most needed a lift. Dinner with him had been a lovely interlude, and there was no denying the intriguing vibes that seemed to pass between them.

Belinda, God rest her, had been right as usual. But then, who but Belinda could possibly have predicted the affinity between her best friend and her boss?

"Sam's like you in so many ways, Paula," she'd told her during one of their Sunday gabfests. *"He likes obscure old love songs and movies and baseball! And*

he's strong and opinionated—even more so than you. He's exactly the kind of man you'd respect. . . ."

Paula looked at the card that had come with Sam's flowers. "You're the top"—it was a phrase from an old love song!

Ah, Belinda! She blinked away tears. *Whatever will I do without you?*

And then she frowned, wondering if Belinda had known anything about the danger of the old refinery site. If she had, she'd never mentioned it to Paula, and that would not have been like Belinda. In fact, Paula realized, if Belinda had suspected that such a health hazard existed, she would have been out there in the community, actively protesting and demanding that the cleanup get under way!

Of course, if Belinda *had* known, then Ted would know, too. Paula could ask him this weekend. She felt her heartbeat quicken a little. She was not looking forward to seeing him. . . .

It occurred to her then that Danny One-Eye was to have been arraigned on Monday. On impulse, she picked up the phone, dialed information, and asked for the number of the public defender's office in Seaview.

Mike Shaffer answered his phone on the first ring, and he sounded surprised to hear from her. "Paula? Well, hello. You've caught me off guard, but . . . I'm glad to have the chance to apologize."

"There's no need to apologize." She knew she sounded imperious. "My behavior the other day was as bad as yours. Actually, I was calling to follow up on the arraignment—Danny went to court yesterday, didn't he?"

There was a slight hesitation. "It went as expected. My client entered a plea of not guilty. The judge ordered psychological testing before binding him over for trial."

Paula hesitated. "The police think he did it."

"Presumably. They took their case to the D.A."

"But you don't think he's guilty."

A pause. "Beside the point. I will be working to mount his defense."

"I know that. That isn't what I asked, Mr. Shaffer. I asked if you think he is guilty."

A longer pause. "The name is Mike. And the answer is no. I don't."

When the doorbell rang, Lissa ran to answer it. Ted could hear Sam's voice.

"Well, hello, sweetheart. How are we today? And how is your friend, Pooh?"

Lissa giggled. "We're okay, Sam. We went to see *your* friend today!"

"You went to see *my* friend?"

"Yes! Dr. Irvin! Didn't you say he's your friend?"

Ted looked up from the soup he was stirring as Sam came into the kitchen with Lissa.

"Ah, yes!" Sam was saying. "So he is. And what did you think of my friend?"

Lissa shrugged. "I like him, I guess. He has lots of stuffed animals, and he said I could play with them anytime I want. Daddy said we can go back."

Ted busied himself with plates. "I was just fixing us some lunch. Care for a bowl of soup and a sandwich?"

Sam shook his head. "I have to go to Denver. I just thought I'd stop by. How're you doing?"

Ted made a face. "All right, I guess. Uh, Lissa, why don't you go wash up for lunch?"

"But my hands are clean!"

"Go wash up anyway. Lunch'll be ready in a minute." He stirred the soup until Lissa had gone. "That half-wit was arraigned yesterday."

"Yes, I know. It was all over the news. Judge ordered psychological testing."

Ted grimaced. "Psychological testing! Whatever happened to victim's rights? Got a little girl here who's lost her mommy. And they're giving him psychological testing!"

Sam started to say something, but Ted cut him off. "I want this trial over with, don't you see? I want to see them hang that bastard from a tree, and then maybe we can get on with our lives!"

"Ted—"

"All clean, Daddy! See? Both hands!"

Ted knew his smile was tight. "Good girl. Come sit down at the table. Sam, are you sure you won't join us?"

"Ah, no. Thanks. I've got a plane to catch. I'll let myself out, all right? Lissa, you take good care of your daddy. I expect I'll be back sometime Friday."

Danny Gentry, if that was his real name, had an IQ of 53, according to Stanford-Binets administered at White Rock Academy when he was four and again at age fourteen.

According to Mike's battered volume of *World Book*, it put Danny on the high end of moderately retarded. It meant that, under the best of conditions, he might be minimally trainable. He could learn some basic language, maybe some math. But apart from sheltered workshop-type tasks, he would likely never develop any skills.

Mike had no idea whether White Rock Academy came close to offering the best of conditions, but from everything he read, it was clear the young Danny Gentry had been a docile, easily managed charge. There was nothing in the file that indicated he had a tendency toward violence or even a volatile temper.

George Tulley, the old gardener, had said as much and indicated that Danny was good with flowers; that the young man who followed him around the grounds had learned to trim bushes and such. Possibly, if Danny had stayed at White Rock until he reached the legal age of eighteen, he might have been mainstreamed into a halfway house or some sort of sheltered workshop program. But if, as the records showed, he'd been released to a relative, then the county had probably relinquished custody. It was easy to understand, once Danny'd left his uncle's home, why he'd ended up on the streets.

Mike was eager to find this uncle and fill in some more of the blanks. He'd already asked a buddy at the Department of Motor Vehicles if he could run down a guy named Gentry in Mendocino. But at this juncture, Mike was well aware, he was already improperly withholding information—information about his client's name and background that he was obligated to share with the police, the court, and the forensic psychologist who was going to be working with Danny.

Putting the *World Book* back in the office bookcase, he drained the last of a cup of coffee, then straightened his tie, put on his jacket and strolled up front to the reception area.

"I'm heading over to the police station and then to the jail," he told a new, bleached-blond receptionist.

She fixed him with a wet-lipped smile that put his senses on alert, but then the notion struck that he was in no mood to flit from one Gloria to another. Nodding benignly, he turned on his heel and took the steps downstairs two at a time.

The police department was housed on the upper floors of the same stucco box that housed the jail. Mike took the stairs up and turned left to the Investigative Section.

Harvey Nattlinger took his feet off the desk and grunted a rude greeting.

Mike responded in kind, fingering a dusty, plastic philodendron, Harvey's sole concession to ambience. "Came to talk about Danny One-Eye."

"Yep. Figured as much. . . . AKA Danny Gentry. That what you came to tell me?"

Mike allowed himself a slow smile. "You already picked that up?"

Nattlinger shrugged. "That's what they pay me for. How come you didn't disclose it yesterday?"

"I'll tell you that if you tell me how you got it."

"What is this, quid pro quo? I got it from the suspect."

"No you didn't."

"Okay. I got it from Garza. He did some follow-up, found somebody who knew the guy—a kid who went through county with him."

Mike was incredulous. "Felipe Garza did some follow-up. I thought he had his case nailed shut. Motive. Method. Opportunity. A confession, for Pete's sake! I saw his report. So what's he doing follow-up for? . . . Or isn't his case nailed shut?"

Nattlinger opened a desk drawer. "The D.A. took it, didn't he?" He rummaged around and came up with a Mars Bar. "You want a half of this?"

Mike was beginning to pick up something curious, but you didn't push Harvey around. He took a seat on a plastic chair. "No. Thanks. So what do you think about Gentry?"

"You owe me one, Shaffer. Why didn't you disclose?"

"I'd only just gotten it—wasn't even positive. I wanted some time to check him out."

Nattlinger chomped down hard on the candy bar and took his time chewing. "Hey, man, you read the report. No priors, no prints, no rap sheet. State never heard of Danny Gentry—no One-Eye, Two-Eye, Three-Eye."

Mike nodded slowly. "So why does he turn around and take a knife to a woman in her kitchen?"

"Hell, buddy boy. You read the report. Even a moron has a sex drive."

"Come on, Harvey, it doesn't wash."

"The prosecutor will say it does."

"Then the prosecutor's wrong."

"The kid was carrying one of the dead woman's earrings in his pocket. What is that, some kind of a fetish? She didn't give him one earring."

"So he found it! Hell, I don't know where he got it. It doesn't make him her killer."

Nattlinger munched the other half of the Mars Bar. "It might if you got no defense."

Mike stood up. "We'll have a defense."

"Yeah? You gonna put him on the stand? Your best defense is no defense, buddy boy. You better find yourself another viable suspect."

Mike's eyes narrowed. "That's your job, Harvey."

"Yeah. Well, not anymore. Case closed. The lieutenant's happy. The D.A. is satisfied. Hell, even the media's happy."

Mike thought about Paula Carroll's phone call. She hadn't sounded happy. She sounded like a woman with something on her mind. He had a feeling they'd be talking again. . . . He took a shot in the dark. "So where do I look, Harve?"

"What am I, a crystal ball?"

"The husband? Husbands are a good place to start. What do you think about the husband, Harvey?"

No answer.

"Oops. Sorry. Overstepped my bounds. I know. We're playing on different teams."

"It's a long season, buddy boy. What the hell? Make a run at the pennant."

CHAPTER
~13~

Poise and self-confidence were Paula's long suits, but on Thursday they seemed to have deserted her. She fussed with her hair far longer than usual, and she had a hard time deciding what to wear.

She'd finally decided on a navy linen suit that seemed to her both youthful and sophisticated. But now, as she turned in front of her dressing room mirror, she wished she had decided on the green.

"Oh, come on, Paula," she mumbled to herself. "It's only Zach and some cretin producer. And anyway, you could do far worse than reading the news on KSFO, the best of the Bay, for the rest of your natural life!"

Spraying a fine mist of *L'Air du Temps*, she picked up her handbag and coat, then nearly collided with Deirdre Adams as she stepped out into the narrow hallway.

"Deirdre, sorry." She patted her arm. "When I'm late, I'm like a ship at full steam."

"Well, you look fabulous." Deirdre's dark eyes were mischievous. "Whoever he is, I hope he's worth it."

She had told no one about her meeting today—or the fact that a network news show was courting her. In show biz, as in baseball, there was no sure thing, and it was never over till it was over. Still, she felt the slightest sting of disloyalty and that was probably what kept her talking. "How's the Seaview refinery story coming? Have you managed to get to that—what's his name? Davidson?"

Deirdre shook her head. "No, and department heads at the Department of Health don't seem willing to talk to me either. It's like we've come across some kind of sacred cow or something, and everybody wants to look the other way. I take it you haven't turned up anything."

"No, but there are a few more people I can talk to. I'm going back up to Seaview this weekend. And I can make a few phone calls. Tell me, Deirdre, when did this whole thing begin to surface?"

"As nearly as I can tell, some worried people in Seaview began reporting the pollution nearly two years ago. But for some reason or other, it was only just recently that the state finally got involved—and by that time, the owners had filed bankruptcy and washed their hands of the whole mess."

Something ominous flirted with Paula's brain and lodged coldly in her stomach. But there was no time to think about it now. She had to go and sparkle in the spotlight.

Excusing herself with a promise to get back to her, Paula left Deirdre in the hall and managed to catch an elevator in mid-route, a trick not easily mastered.

Outside, on Powell Street, a chill wind blew and the skies above looked threatening. Paula looked dubiously at a burgundy-colored cable car and then decided to flag a cab to Fisherman's Wharf.

The lunchtime crowds, as always, were enormous, tourists and San Franciscans alike munching on fresh clams or shrimp cocktails as they strolled the brick-lined walkways. Paula threaded her way past dozens of open-air stalls, breathing in the scent of raw fish and sourdough bread, to the landmark restaurant that was Alioto's.

She spotted Zach at a window table at the same moment he saw her. He rose to greet her, coming barely to her shoulders, and his silky white mustache grazed her cheek.

"Hello, Zach."

"Paula Carroll, this is Stu Snyder. Stu, you know Paula, of course."

"Of course." The other man took her hand. "My dear, you are even more vibrant in person."

Snyder was short and nearly bald, with a round, pink face. Paula smiled at him as she slid into her seat and arranged her things next to her. "I'm delighted to meet you," she told the cherub-faced producer. "I'm a big fan of 'Bay Area News.'"

He looked at her, smiling, refracted light from the overhead chandelier glinting off his steel-rimmed glasses. "Well, if the proper conditions can be met, we will be pleased to welcome you aboard."

Paula took encouragement from the remark. Zach had not been merely blowing smoke. As for the "proper conditions," whatever they were, she was sure she would find out in due course. Meanwhile, she was determined to enjoy her lunch and the spectacular view of San Francisco Bay.

As it turned out, she needn't have worried. The meeting had not been planned to hammer out details. That was Zach's métier, and he would handle it on his own. Lunch at Alioto's was simply social; an opportunity for Zach to show her off, like a jewel in the setting of his choice.

She played her part masterfully, taking full advantage of her wide smile and expressive eyes. But she saw to it that the conversation remained lively and wide-ranging, so that she had the opportunity to showcase her intellect as well as her physical attributes.

Stu Snyder's pink face was beaming by the time they ordered dessert, and Zach winked at Paula from behind his menu. He didn't need to. She knew it was going well. Her poise and self-confidence were back.

Mike made a detour to the ice cream shop on Blake Street before he went to the jail. But despite the cold weather, the cone was dripping down his wrist by the time he signed himself in.

Dickie Hetherington thought it was a stitch. "Hey, you need some help *licking* that, *counselor?* Or don't they teach you how to do that in law school?"

"It's not for me. It's for Danny, you turkey, and it's not buying favor, it's buying confidence."

He found Danny sitting on his cot, polishing his harmonica with his denim shirttail. For a moment, the ice cream did seem to catch his interest, but Danny's attention span was short and he soon put the cone down on his untouched lunch tray, where it pooled into a sticky, pink mess.

"Danny, look at me," Mike began gently. "We have to have a talk. Do you remember me?"

Danny's head bobbed up and down. "Sure I remember. You're Mike."

"Good! I'm Mike! And you're Danny Gentry. Isn't that right? Not Danny One-Eye. Danny Gentry."

Danny stared at him, slack-jawed, his eyes reflecting his consternation.

"Do you remember when you went away to school at White Rock? You told them your name was Danny Gentry."

The youth's eyes narrowed, and Mike could fairly see the grudging machinations of Danny's brain. Then Danny cocked his head to one side, and something like a smile lit his face. "Yeah!" he said, his voice rising like a child's. "Rock! Danny Gentry go to school!"

Mike was encouraged. "You remember White Rock? You remember going to school there?"

"Sure!" The youth was animated now. "Me and Peter go to school!"

Mike guessed that whoever Peter was, he was the kid Felipe Garza had found; the one who'd told him Danny One-Eye was also known as Danny Gentry. He decided to press his luck. "Who else do you remember? Do you remember your friend George?"

Now Danny was genuinely smiling, revealing large, white teeth. "George, sure! George my friend. Where is George? He's my friend!"

Mike laughed. "George still works at White Rock, Danny. And he remembers you, too. He told me you and he were buddies. You used to help him trim the bushes."

Danny nodded happily. "Yeah! Danny and George trim the bushes."

Mike hesitated. "George told me he was sad when you went away, Danny. Do you remember when you left White Rock? When your uncle came to get you?"

The smile faded. Danny looked blank.

"Your uncle came to get you from White Rock. He took you to Mendocino."

"Mendo-cino," Danny repeated, but it was clear the name meant nothing.

Mike tried again. "Your uncle had a farm. He took you to his farm in Mendocino, didn't he? Do you remember the way it was at the farm, Danny? Do you remember cows and pigs and chickens and horses?"

Danny blinked. His big hands began to fidget. "George. I like to see George."

Mike tried hard not to show his disappointment. He had thought they were making progress. He had hoped if he could somehow win Danny's confidence, he might get him to open up—maybe, with luck, to express what he remembered of the events leading up to Belinda's death.

Now he wasn't sure about it. He had the distinct feeling he was playing out of his league. He hadn't the training—and maybe not the patience—to deal effectively with someone like Danny.

Then a strange thing happened. Danny reached over and patted Mike's arm. His dark eyes seemed full of pain. "Mike . . . sad," he murmured.

Mike stared at him. "No, Danny. Really. I'm not sad."

Danny's big head bobbed up and down. "That's okay. Danny One-Eye be your friend."

It was past three when the cabbie left Paula in front of the KSFO building, and she knew she'd have to study her script while Rollie did her makeup if she was going to be ready for the five o'clock broadcast.

Hurrying inside, she took the elevator up and collected a copy of her script from Betty Lou. Then she dashed into her dressing room for a minute to freshen up before heading over to Makeup.

She had no intention of making the call until the moment she picked up the telephone—and even then, she had to force herself to flip through her personal phone book. But when she found the number for Todd Hazeltine, her fingers seemed to punch in the series of numbers almost of their own accord.

Todd had been a newswriter at KVKW, a tiny radio station near Ventura where Paula had found her first broadcasting job. He'd had hopes of moving into broadcasting, too, but he'd had neither a truly distinctive voice nor the fortitude to bide his time. What he did have was a wife and a baby, and when he heard of a job opening in the state's public relations office, he applied without hesitation.

No one had been more surprised than he when he actually got the job, but he must have done well at it because he started out writing press releases and kept moving up through the ranks. The last time Paula'd seen him had been at a press party a year ago when he'd been named public information officer.

Paula would have been willing to bet that Deirdre had elected to bypass Todd's office in her search for information on the refinery cleanup. Whether or not they were privy to the facts, PIOs were paid to stick to the "party line" when discussing sensitive issues with the media, and Deirdre—like any reporter worth her salt—would have figured she'd get no place with Todd.

But Paula was not interested in pursuing the reasons why the state was not anxious to clean up the mess. At this point, anyway, there was only one little thing she wanted to know.

CHAPTER
14

Traffic was light after the late Friday broadcast, but if it were not for Lissa, Paula wasn't sure she could have geared herself up to make the drive to Seaview after all.

Once, as a child, she'd gone to the supermarket with her mother and though she'd been warned against it, she had plucked out a can of green beans from the middle of a towering display. There was a split second when time and motion had seemed to stand absolutely still, and then—in the time it took Paula to duck around the corner into the cookie aisle—she'd heard a faint rumble and then a hair-raising clatter as cans of green beans crashed down in every direction.

She had tried to laugh, but she'd found her giddiness quickly supplanted with guilt, and although she had never confessed to the deed, she thought of it to this day as a turning point in her life; the moment when she'd understood the meaning of decency and her moral obligation to uphold it.

Now she felt as though she were about to relive the whole, ugly experience, for in challenging Ted she would be plucking at the center of their odd but carefully forged relationship—the fragile support system that had bound Ted to his wife and, by extension, to his wife's best friend.

And then, of course, there was Lissa to consider, beautiful little Lissa, the tiny wonder whose very birth had seemed like a minor miracle.

Paula concentrated on a curve in the road, loath to dredge up more memories. But it seemed there was scarcely a corner of her life that did not involve Belinda. . . .

Paula had stayed late at play rehearsal one night just before the university's *Spring Follies*. The dorm was quiet when she'd signed in and taken the elevator upstairs, but she'd heard Belinda's anguished sobs as she was letting herself into their room.

Belinda was sprawled face down across her bed, crying into her pillow. Paula was so stunned she'd just stood there for a minute, debating what to do.

Finally she'd sat on the edge of the bed and tentatively patted Belinda's arm, and Belinda had jumped up and turned to stare at her, dabbing uselessly at red-rimmed eyes.

"Oh, God, Paula." Sniffle. *"I had no idea—"* Sob. *"I mean, I didn't know when you'd be home. . . ."*

"What difference does that make? Belinda, what on earth is wrong?"

It had taken a while, but Belinda finally told her. She'd been to see the doctor for her blood tests, and the doctor had suggested, since she was going to be married, that she have an internal exam.

"The p-peritonitis," she'd managed between sobs.

"R-remember when my appendix ru–ruptured—when we were k-kids?"

Paula'd nodded mutely and, through her tears, Belinda had managed to tell her that the peritonitis had apparently caused an inflammation of the lining of her abdominal wall. The scarring it had left might make it difficult—maybe even impossible, the doctor said—for Belinda to become pregnant.

Paula didn't know what she'd expected, but in a way it was almost a relief. *"God, Belinda, I thought you were going to tell me you were dying of some stupid, rare disease."*

But Belinda had not been comforted. *"Paula, you don't understand! H-how am I going to tell Ted? We've talked so often—I mean, we both want ch-children. How am I going to tell him?"*

The question had preceded another round of wailing, and Paula had waited for it to subside. Then she'd taken her by the shoulders and forced Belinda to look at her and kept her voice quiet so Belinda would have to listen.

"Look, Belinda, this is a little premature. I mean, the whole thing is still a maybe. Right? Belinda, isn't that what you said? You might *not be able to get pregnant?"*

Belinda had nodded. *"But—what about Ted?"*

"Tell him! Of course, you have to tell him. But I guarantee you, he loves you so much he won't care if you don't have children."

Paula had taken a little liberty there. She really didn't know Ted all that well. Suppose Belinda told him and he said, "Well, that's that," and called off the whole darned wedding?

So Paula'd held her breath for the next few weeks, until she couldn't stand the suspense anymore. And when she finally asked, Belinda'd smiled shyly and told her how wonderful Ted was.

"He told me I was silly even to worry even for one minute—that if we wanted a baby badly enough, we would have one. And you were right, Paula. He said he loved me so much that it really wouldn't matter, anyway!"

Paula groaned. And this was the man she now believed might have murdered Belinda in cold blood! . . .

She brushed away tears as the lights of Seaview rose up in the distance. . . .

It was after eleven when Mike Shaffer returned to the Seaview Jail. Dickie Hetherington was nowhere in sight, and he did not know the night jailer, a beer-bellied giant with a craggy face and a nose that rambled all over it.

"I want to see Danny Gentry," Mike said, scrawling his name in the log. "I'm his attorney, Mike Shaffer."

The man blinked. "You gotta be kidding. It was lights out over two hours ago."

"I know it's late." Mike stood his ground. "But I'd like to see Danny if he's awake."

The jailer shrugged and slowly roused himself out of a well-worn, padded armchair. Mike figured the guy must have hauled it in himself. It sure wasn't city-issue.

Bare lightbulbs hanging from the ceiling gave the butter-colored walls a sickly pallor, and footsteps seemed to echo more loudly on the concrete than they did in the light of day.

Mike had gone back to the office after dinner hoping to get some time alone on the computer, and he'd found the message from Harrison Jellick, his friend at the DMV:

Located a Martin Gentry just outside of Mendocino. If you care, he owns an '82 Ford pickup. His phone number, whether you care or not, is 627–4890.

Mike had looked up the area code for Mendocino and quickly dialed the number. The guy who answered sounded cranky. "Yeah. Martino Vineyards."

Martino Vineyards. It was worth a try. "I'm looking for Martin Gentry."

"Yeah? Who wants him?"

Several scenarios played themselves out in Mike's head. Finally he said, "I'm calling on behalf of his nephew, Danny Gentry."

Wrong choice.

The guy hung up.

Mike shrugged and turned on the computer. But no matter how he tried to focus, his concentration was shot.

He'd been doing fine that afternoon prodding Danny's memory, until he came to the part about his uncle. Then Danny'd shut off, and now Mike thought he might just understand why. He'd been asking Danny about his uncle's farm, evoking images of horses and pigs and chickens. But Martin Gentry—if that's who he'd spoken to—apparently owned some kind of winery. Likely, he had no pigs and chickens. Just grapes. Lots of grapes.

Mike had every intention of waiting till morning to question Danny again. But somehow or other, here he stood now, staring into the jail cell at nearly midnight, listening to his client snuffle in his sleep, making little, mewling noises like a child.

But he hadn't been standing there more than a minute when Danny sat up on his cot, clutching at his blanket but wary and alert, as though he knew he was being watched.

It was the reaction of a street person, Mike realized, maybe the only hope for self-protection—that well-developed sense that someone was watching, maybe coveting what little you had.

But in the next instant Danny recognized him and gave him a toothy grin. "Mike!" He threw the blanket aside. It could as easily have been noon as midnight.

Ted greeted her with a familiar hug, but Paula could feel the tension in his body—a force as palpable as an electric charge. It first surprised and then alarmed her.

"Hi." She tried to smile, setting down her things. "How are you? Are you all right?"

"I'm fine," he told her, looking just past her shoulder. "Lissa, too. She's fine. I've had her to see your Dr. Irvin. She seems to like him all right."

Paula hesitated. He was not *her* Dr. Irvin. But she was glad he'd taken Lissa to see him. "Good." She sat lightly in a corner of the sofa. "I'm looking forward to seeing her."

There was an awkward pause, which Ted tried to fill by moving Paula's bags to the stairwell. "You must be tired," he murmured.

"Yes, I guess I am. But this seems like such a good time to talk. With Lissa in bed, and no distractions." She gestured toward the easy chair across from her.

He sat in the chair, his spine straight. "What did you want to talk about?"

She looked at him, this stranger in faded chinos, a stranger with a friend's face. "I'm working on a story," she said evenly. "I thought you might be able to help."

A pause. "What?"

"I need some information. I'm hoping maybe you can help."

Ted blinked. "A story. What about?"

She watched him closely. "The old refinery here in Seaview. The state's declared it a public danger. But then, of course, you know that."

A range of emotions seemed to play across his face. She could see him struggling to choose the right one. "Yes," he said finally. "Of course I know. I did the site inspection several months ago."

"I know." Paula nodded. "Nearly *two years* after the city asked the state to look into it."

Ted threw up his hands. "Come on, Paula, you know the way these things operate. Paperwork. Logjams. More work than staff. Good old American bureaucracy."

"And Lissa in school within shouting distance of all this horrendous contamination!"

"Paula—"

"My God, Ted, how could you allow it? Why did you drag your feet? It's almost as though you were *waiting* until the owners had a chance to slip off the hook!"

Ted stood up. "Oh, come on, Paula—"

"Tell me that wasn't it. Tell me you didn't drag your feet, Ted. Tell me you didn't know what was happening!"

He flushed. "Paula, I had no idea—not when the

whole thing started. It wasn't until we got into the site that I realized what a pesthole it was."

She looked at him levelly. "Did Belinda know?"

He hesitated. "Yes. Not at first. But then she got involved. You know Belinda. She was spearheading some kind of parents' group."

It took every ounce of restraint she could muster for Paula to stop right there. But she was not yet ready to accuse him of collusion—much less of anything more sinister. "I see,"—she rubbed the back of her neck—"I guess I should have realized that." She stood. "And you're right. It's late and I'm tired. I think I'll go up to bed."

Ted appeared more puzzled than relieved that she'd stopped the frontal attack. He nodded slowly as she moved toward the stairs. "Right. See you in the morning. I haven't been sleeping well these days. I think I'll stay up. Maybe watch Letterman for a while."

Paula went through the automatic motions of getting ready for bed, creaming her face and brushing her hair as her mind raced to put together what she knew and what she suspected.

Belinda had clearly been bothered about something. She'd talked about a problem involving Ted. What if she knew that her husband had been willing to trade a whole town's welfare for—what, some kind of payoff? If she'd threatened to expose him—even to leave him—would that have moved him to murder?

And even if it had, would he dare tip his hand by making a phone call to scare Paula off? In any case, Ted knew her well—well enough to know that kind of ploy would never keep her away. . . .

She was brushing her teeth when something else

occurred to her, and she stopped in mid-stroke. Her mailbox! Maybe Belinda had suspected that Ted was . . . losing his grip. Maybe she *had* mailed something to Paula—some kind of proof, some kind of warning. If Ted suspected, would he—could he—have driven to San Francisco to retrieve it?

Paula straightened up and stared into the mirror. The morning of Belinda's burial, Paula had awakened to find a note from Ted. *"Couldn't sleep. Went for a drive. . . ."*

When, Ted? Early enough to drive to San Francisco and back? Early enough to ravage my mailbox and be back before the morning was over?

She closed her eyes. *Help me, Belinda. Tell me what to do next. . . .*

When the thought came into her head, she turned off the tap, stepped into the hall and listened from the top of the stairs. She could hear muted sounds coming from the television, music, a peal of laughter. For all she knew, Ted had fallen asleep. Or he could come upstairs at any minute. Still, once the decision was made, she knew she was going to go through with it.

Quietly, she made her way down the hall, not to the guest room but to the master bedroom, where a week ago, high on a shelf of the closet, she had seen Belinda's diaries.

Aware of her heartbeat, she slipped into the bedroom, but she did not turn on a light. Her eyes had grown accustomed to the darkness, and if Ted should appear, she decided she would tell him she had come in looking for aspirin. She knew they kept no medicines in the other bathroom, since that was the one Lissa used.

The sliding door of Belinda's closet was closed.

Holding her breath, Paula eased it open. When she had it open no more than a foot, she slipped quietly inside—but when she reached up to the right side of the shelf, her hand encountered nothing.

Perplexed, she groped her way across the length of the shelf, feeling for purses, hatboxes. But there was nothing, and when she put her hands out in front of her, she felt only a tangle of empty hangers.

No! she heard herself scream silently, slapping at the hangers in frustration.

Then the lights snapped on, and when Paula spun around, she was staring into Ted's angry face.

CHAPTER

—15—

Paula wasn't sure whether Ted had believed her story about wandering through the wrong door looking for aspirin. What she did know was that she was as dismayed to find out that he had disposed of Belinda's things as he was to find her in his wife's closet.

"You might at least have asked me, Ted, if there was anything of Belinda's I wanted," she'd told him, hoping she sounded more wounded than angry.

But Ted would have none of it, telling Paula he felt it was best—for Lissa's sake as well as his own—to empty the house of heartbreaking memories and try to get on with their lives. He had set aside Belinda's few pieces of jewelry for Lissa, he said, and told the Salvation Army they could have whatever was left in return for clearing out the closet.

In a small way, Paula really was hurt. She and Belinda had been best friends since childhood, and since Belinda had no other relatives, Ted might have realized that Paula was the logical one to decide what to keep and what not to keep.

But, in the end, she knew she was most upset that Belinda's diaries had gone with the rest—mainly because they might have provided a clue about the state of her relationship with Ted. She could try calling the Salvation Army, of course, but it wasn't likely they had opted to keep anything quite so personal as diaries.

So Paula had merely clamped her lips together and marched out of the bedroom—without the aspirin. And now, this morning, Ted was noticeably cool to her as they sat with Lissa at the breakfast table.

"Guess what, Paula?" Lissa sprinkled cinnamon on her oatmeal. "I get to go back to nursery school on Monday!"

Paula looked at Ted for confirmation. He nodded, concentrating on his cereal. "We've got to get back into a routine sometime," he mumbled. "Might as well be now."

Paula hesitated, knowing that, at some point soon, she was going to want to discuss with Ted what plans he had for Lissa's future. For the moment, she supposed he would resume the same schedule that Belinda had so carefully organized.

"Everything will go on the way it was," Ted went on, confirming what Paula was thinking. "Judy will pick up Lissa along with her daughter on the nights they go to gymnastics class. On the other three nights, I'll pick up both girls on my way home from the office."

Paula smiled at Lissa. "That's wonderful, honey. I'll bet your teacher will be happy to see you."

They were clearing the dishes and loading the dishwasher when Ted came up behind them. "It's been more than a week since I've been to my office. I'll be there on Monday, of course. But I wonder if you'd mind if I went in for a while this morning— just to look through the mail and get organized."

Paula would not have minded if he had told her he was leaving on an extended trip to Madagascar. And besides, the prospect of spending some time alone with Lissa had more than a little appeal. "Of course." She flashed Ted her on-camera smile. "Take as long as you like."

He hadn't been gone more than a few minutes when the phone rang. Lissa ran to answer it. "Hi, Sam," she piped. "Daddy isn't home. I'm pretending Paula is my mommy."

Paula blinked, taking the phone, and sent Lissa upstairs to dress. "Hi." She sat at the kitchen table. "Ted just left for his office."

"Oh. I'm in Denver. I thought I'd be back today, but I can't get away before Monday. And Ted looked so—I don't know—rocky, when I stopped by the other day, I thought I'd check and see how things are going."

Paula hesitated, wishing Sam were there. "He's lucky to have you for a friend. To tell the truth, I am a little worried. We can talk more about it when I see you."

"Yes," Sam agreed. "I was planning to call you, anyway. I've managed to get something for you."

"What?"

"Wynn Davidson's home number. The head of Duncan Associates?"

"Sam, that's wonderful! How did you do it?"

"The world isn't all that big. I had to cash in a couple of medium-sized favors, but if it makes you happy, it's worth it."

Paula reached for a notepad and pencil and scribbled down the number. "Thanks. I owe you one."

"And I plan to collect. How about dinner on Thursday? I'll be in San Francisco. Can I call you at the station?"

"Please do. I'll be looking forward to it."

She put the slip of paper in her pants pocket, intending to pass it on to Deirdre. Then she said her good-byes and headed up the stairs to see how Lissa was doing.

But the familiar aroma of Belinda's perfume assailed her halfway up, and she had to lean against the banister for a minute before she proceeded upstairs.

Lissa was standing in front of her mirror, dressed in blue corduroy, splashing little pools of perfume behind her ears and onto the insides of her wrists.

"Lissa!" Paula cried, and the child flinched and shoved the perfume bottle in a drawer, turning, white-faced, to stare at Paula with wide, frightened eyes.

Paula didn't know whether to laugh or cry, Lissa looked so pitiful and guilty. She bent down and held out her arms. "Honey, where did you find Mommy's perfume?"

Tears spilled from Lissa's azure eyes as she ran into Paula's arms. "It was in her room. I kn-know where she keeps it. They were g-going to take it awaaay. . . ."

"Who was going to take it?"

"The S-Sabbation Army! They were t-taking all my mommy's stuff!"

Paula could only guess how devastated Lissa must have been to see strangers packing up Belinda's things. It made her furious to think that Ted had allowed it while Lissa was in the house.

"It's all right, honey." She held Lissa close and breathed in the warm, little girl smell of her. "It just surprised me to smell Mommy's perfume. I know she wouldn't mind that you kept it."

Lissa stopped sobbing and laid one cheek tentatively against Paula's shoulder. "Will Daddy be mad?"

"No, I don't think so. We'll just have to tell him that you have it. And I think"—she brushed the blond curls back—"that it might be a good idea to save it. You know, not to use Mommy's perfume, at least until you're a little bit bigger. What do you think?"

Lissa nodded, heaving one last sigh. "Okay . . . , I guess. . . . Does that mean I can't play with her wedding doll either—or look at the pictures in her Me Box?"

Paula reared back to look at Lissa. "Her wedding doll? And what is a Me Box?"

Lissa's lower lip quivered. "That's the only other stuff I took. . . . Mommy said I could have the doll someday—and the Me Box is just like mine!"

Paula frowned. "Show me, Lissa."

Lissa hesitated for a minute, then ran to her closet, crouched down and pulled out a gray and white carton.

The moment Paula saw the carton, she remembered the doll inside it—a handmade bridal doll dressed in white lace and satin that Belinda had received as a shower gift. She smiled, fingering the tiny wedding veil, but she felt angry all over again at Ted for the cavalier way in which he had chosen to dispose of his dead wife's possessions. "Oh, yes," she said. "I remember this now. Mommy really liked that doll. And you're right. She would have wanted you to have it, if you promise to take good care of it."

Lissa's head bobbed happily. "I promise. I'll hardly even look at it!" She bent down again and rummaged around in the far corner of her closet, coming up finally with two heart-shaped boxes that looked as though they might once have held candy.

She held out the smaller, pink one for Paula to see. "See? This is Lissa's Me Box! Mommy said I could put stuff in it that I want to keep forever and ever!"

Paula smiled. It was like Belinda to put a high value on privacy—to give Lissa a box of her own in which to save what was meaningful. "I see," she said softly. "And Mommy had a Me Box, too?"

Lissa held out the larger, red box. "She kept it in her dresser! Once I saw her take it out and put some stuff inside."

Oh, Belinda! Paula struggled with a host of colliding emotions—love, loyalty, pride, grief—even anger that Belinda had succumbed, leaving a hole in all their lives. But Lissa was watching her with frank curiosity, and she tried for a reassuring smile.

"Do you have a Me Box?" Lissa's voice was a whisper.

Paula shook her head. "No."

"Do you want one?"

She brushed away a tear. "I don't know. I don't know what I'd put inside."

Lissa seemed to waver. Then she thrust out the red box. "You can have my Mommy's if you want."

Paula blinked. "You want me to have it?"

The child nodded soberly.

Paula thought it was the most treasured gift that anyone could ever have given her. She opened her arms again, and Lissa ran into them and she held her very close.

A thin cloud cover obscured the sun, but Mike felt the heat of it on his back. He was perspiring lightly as he crossed the arroyo and jogged down the hillside toward town.

He'd spent the morning going over his notes on every meeting he'd had with Danny Gentry, from the first, almost incoherent interview through the talk they'd had in the jail late last night. Mike was convinced the hulking youth was beginning to like him—to trust him—and that soon, very soon, he'd be able to tell him what had happened in Belinda Raymond's kitchen.

Of course, even if he believed Danny was innocent, proving it was going to be tough. The kid might not be a credible witness even if he were able to take the stand, and the evidence against him—both physical and circumstantial—was going to be hard to refute.

He crossed Blake, uncomfortably aware of the T-shirt sticking to his back, the rivulets of sweat that ran the length of his spine and collected in the waistband of his running shorts.

He had a decent character witness in old George Tulley, who would describe Danny as a gentle soul, and—long shot—he was hoping the psychologist might get the same opinion from Danny's uncle.

Of course, it would help if Mike could throw a spotlight on another viable suspect. But despite Harvey Nattlinger's oblique implication that the husband might be fair game, it was going to be tough to prove that Ted Raymond's relationship with his wife had been anything but idyllic—and beyond that, Mike was forced to admit, he didn't have a clue where to look.

Out-and-out frustration and a parched throat seemed to propel him toward the ice cream shop. He was half a block away when he saw Paula, and he stopped to admire the view.

She was bending toward the little girl, her sleek, tawny hair swinging free, lithe and graceful in khaki-colored pants and a print shirt knotted at her waist.

If she saw him, she gave no sign of recognition. She and the child went into the ice cream shop. Mike debated for a minute, then mopped his face with a Kleenex and jogged the half block to the store.

"Hi there." He turned toward the little girl. "Great day for an ice cream."

She studied him. "I know you. You came to my house on my birthday."

Paula turned then, her blue eyes wary. "Mr. Shaffer."

"Mike. Hello, Paula."

"Lissa, honey, what would you like? Chocolate chip? Is that still your favorite?"

The little girl nodded, and Paula spoke to the clerk. "Two chocolate chip cones. Double scoops."

When the ice cream came, to Mike's utter surprise, she did not hurry away. He ordered, and as he turned to go, she fell into step beside him. Outside the shop, Lissa walked very slowly, carefully licking her cone. Mike and Paula stopped and waited for her.

"How's your case going?" Paula sounded casual.

"Fine." He tried to look away, but he found himself mesmerized by her small, pink tongue as it curled around the ice cream.

"I spoke with someone in the D.A.'s office. He still thinks they have a solid case against Danny."

"No doubt." Mike tried to concentrate on his cone. "It doesn't mean they're correct."

"And if they aren't . . ." She seemed to be searching for words. "You still think it . . . might have been . . . her husband."

He turned to look at her, wondering what it was he was picking up in her voice. "I haven't discounted anything yet. As far as I'm concerned, anything is possible."

When Lissa caught up with them, they walked for a moment in total silence.

"Paula, my feet hurt," Lissa whined.

"Oh, Lissa, we haven't walked that far."

"Yes we have, and they hurt."

Without thinking, Mike turned to Paula and handed her his ice cream cone. Then he bent down, swooped the little girl up, and sat her on his shoulders.

Lissa squealed with delight. Paula looked alarmed. Mike grinned, took back his ice cream cone, and forced her to fall back into stride.

"Look, Paula! I'm bigger than you!" The child bounced on his shoulders.

"You certainly seem to have a way with children!"

He smiled. "I'm the oldest of five."

Paula nodded. "Oh, yes. I have a vague memory of the Shaffer brothers—Seaview Little League's secret weapon."

He laughed, absurdly happy that she admitted recalling *anything* about him. He decided not to press his luck. He just kept walking.

"Look!" The little girl bounced up and down. "I can see the tower from here!"

He looked up to see where she was pointing. "I think she means the old refinery. It's closed down, did you know? The state's declared it a public danger. Environmental hazards."

"I know. Don't you find it frightening? Living so close to it, I mean. Belinda—I think Belinda was frightened. Or maybe she was just angry."

"What makes you say that?"

A short pause. "Ted mentioned she was organizing some sort of parents' group—probably to put some pressure on the state to get in there and clean it up."

Mike thought a minute. "Wasn't there some conflict over who was fiscally responsible?"

"Yes." Paula nodded. "The owners of record had declared bankruptcy and abandoned it. Knowing Belinda, she wouldn't have cared who owned it. She would just have wanted it cleaned up."

But somebody might have cared. Mike stopped in his tracks. *Somebody might have cared—a lot. . . .*

CHAPTER

—16—

It was nearly midnight before Paula was alone in the pale peach guest room.

They'd had pizza for dinner—Lissa's all-time favorite—and Lissa had been in bed by eight-thirty, tired after their long afternoon walk. But at ten she had awakened, thrashing in her bed and screaming for her mommy.

It was the first time since the night of Belinda's death that Paula had heard the child screaming, though Ted told her it had happened on another night when she'd been nearly impossible to soothe.

Tonight Lissa had clung to Paula and begged her to stay by her side, and Paula had stayed, singing and telling stories until Lissa fell into a deep, exhausted sleep.

Then Paula'd gone downstairs to sit with Ted for a while, hoping to draw him into conversation. But he had withdrawn from her, focusing—or seeming to focus—on some excruciatingly unfunny television comedy, and finally Paula had said good-night and climbed the stairs again.

Now she stretched out on the Quaker lace coverlet, trying to sort out her thoughts. But the first thing she thought of was the red, heart-shaped box that Lissa had called Belinda's Me-Box, and she got out of bed, retrieved the box from her suitcase and settled down in the armchair.

For a minute, she held the box in her lap, reluctant to look inside. But, knowing Belinda, she could almost guess at the kinds of things she would have saved—and besides, Paula realized, this was very likely all she would ever have to remember her by. Steeling herself, she set the lid aside and began to rummage through the box.

As she'd expected, there were photographs, lots of them, some nearly thirty years old: Belinda with her parents, with her beagle pup, Nuisance, and with Paula on their first day of kindergarten. Paula stared at their childish faces, hers impish and Belinda's so serious, and wondered not for the first time what had knit them so closely together. To all appearances she and Belinda had been as different as day from night. Yet it was as if each of them had brought to the other some missing piece of herself.

There were a couple of especially good report cards and a program from their high school graduation; a yellowing folder listing Belinda Talmadge as valedictorian and Paula as salutatorian. Paula smiled, remembering the rivalry of their junior and senior years. In the end, Belinda had beaten her for the top honor by a measly fraction of a percentage point, and Mrs. Talmadge had taken them out and treated them both to chocolate ice cream sodas.

There was a little tooth, perhaps the very first one

that Belinda had ever lost, and the hospital wrist-band she must have worn when she'd had her ruptured appendix out—and there, in a tiny, double-sided locket was a picture of Belinda and Ted on their wedding day, and one of Lissa, only days old, when they'd taken her home from the hospital.

She found a small envelope containing a copy of the birth announcement they'd sent to all their friends and a larger envelope with a miniature photocopy of Belinda's college transcript.

Then she found another envelope, not nearly as yellowed as the others, and she frowned, perplexed, when she opened it up and saw the letter inside.

It was apparently a copy Belinda had kept of a letter she had written. It was neatly typed on personal stationery—and addressed to Mr. Wynn Elliot Davidson, president, Duncan Associates.

The letter spoke of Belinda's grave concern over the matter of the abandoned refinery and her intention to use every means at her disposal to expose the deception Davidson's company had employed in order to shirk its obligations.

Among those means, Belinda had written, were a vocal and influential parents' group—and the skills and resources of her best friend, San Francisco television reporter Paula Carroll.

Paula read the letter again, and a chill snaked up her spine. It had been written five days before Belinda's death.

It was dreary on Sunday, the kind of monochromatic gray that almost always meant rain was on the way. But it wasn't raining yet, and Mike was determined to make the most of the morning.

He toasted two bagels, slathered them with cream

cheese and arranged them neatly on a plate. Then he poured a glass of orange juice and a big mug of coffee and carried them out to the deck.

He had just put his feet up on the railing and opened the Sunday comics when he heard the muted sound of the telephone calling to him from the kitchen.

For a few seconds he managed to ignore it, but in the end its insistence won out. He got to his feet, took a sip of coffee, and opened the sliding glass door.

"Yeah." He hoped he sounded surly enough to discourage conversation. But the minute he heard the voice on the other end of the line, he knew it was a dead loss.

"Mike, it's Celia. Celia Schwartz. How in the world are you? I hated to call you at home on a Sunday, but it seems we've got this mutual client, and as I recall, you're as bad as I am about working weekends anyway."

Mike grinned, leaning against the doorjamb. "Celia Schwartz, crack psychologist. How are you, Celia? Don't tell me. Let me guess. You're doing the workup on Danny Gentry."

Celia laughed, the same hearty chuckle he remembered from their days in high school, when everybody teased her about having a voice that was twice the size of her waistline. She'd grown into the voice since her marriage to Lou Schwartz, who was supposed to be a fabulous cook, but she retained the energy and the zest for life that Mike remembered so fondly.

"Right!" she trilled. "He's an interesting study. And he likes you. I guess you know that. Anyway, for that amazing bit of deduction, you win a fabulous prize."

"Oh, yeah? What's that?"

Celia chuckled again. "A trip to Mendocino. With me."

Mike shifted his position in the doorway. "The uncle?"

"You win again. A missing link. It could be valuable. And it will give us a chance to compare notes."

He could have argued that he didn't have the time, but Celia wouldn't believe him, and anyway, he was curious about this uncle who'd appeared out of the blue and then dropped out of sight again. In the end, he agreed to meet Celia on Tuesday and make the two-hour trip together.

By the time he sent regards to Lou and the kids and got back out to the deck, his coffee was cold and a brazen wren was pecking away at his bagel.

It was past five in the evening and drizzling steadily when Paula got into her car, more relieved than she could ever remember being to be leaving Belinda's house.

From the moment she'd found the letter to Wynn Davidson, a number of things had made sense:

Belinda's distress.

"Is something wrong?"

"Yes. I guess you could say that. . . ."

The phone call warning Paula to stay away from Seaview. Even the ravaged mailbox.

Paula waved to Lissa, who was watching her from the window, a forlorn little figure beside the draperies, and she wavered, torn between her need to sort things out and her desire to be there for the child.

Lissa had been, if not her sunny little self, at least calm and reasonable all day, seeming—or maybe choosing—not to recall the horrors that had wakened her in the night. Around Paula she was talkative and affectionate, even when she spoke about Belinda. But around Ted she was quiet, almost tentative, and Paula found that disturbing.

Of course, Ted did not invite conversation, Paula admitted, as she backed out of the driveway—not with Lissa, who needed him now more than ever, and certainly not with her. The grief he'd displayed on the night of Belinda's death had evaporated with astonishing speed, leaving him tense, irritable, and unwilling to discuss whatever he was thinking or feeling.

But there'd been more than personal troubles between Belinda and Ted, Paula was now convinced, turning on her headlights and picking up speed as she drove onto the southbound highway. The problems Belinda had alluded to on the telephone had something to do with the refinery, and if Paula could just fit the pieces together, it might shed new light on Belinda's murder.

It was raining harder. Paula adjusted the windshield wipers and moved into the right-hand lane, prepared to travel at a lesser speed on the darkened, rain-slick highway.

Why had Ted dragged his feet on the site inspection? What was his relationship with Wynn Davidson? What had Belinda known? What had she guessed? And which of the men had wanted her dead in order to keep her mouth shut?

Paula didn't know when she first became aware of the car traveling on her left, a big, dark vehicle with tinted windows that hovered just within her line of sight. But it made her nervous and she slowed her pace, expecting that the driver would pass her.

She found herself thinking about Danny One-Eye.

What was his part in all this? Of course, he had not engineered Belinda's death or telephoned Paula or destroyed her mailbox. But had he been persuaded—by Davidson? by Ted?—to commit the actual murder? Or was he, as Mike Shaffer apparently believed, merely a victim of circumstance?

It was embarrassing to remember how she'd railed against Mike when he'd first knocked on Belinda's door, how furious she'd been at the very notion that Ted could in any way be suspect. She sighed. Mike was apparently a decent man, a man with the courage of his convictions. Though he tried to hide it, he was obviously attracted to her, and he'd been wonderful the day before with Lissa! Paula smiled. He was no Sam Pierce, but she clearly owed him an apology. . . .

When she felt the first bump, she inhaled sharply, thinking she'd hit something on the road. When she felt the second, she realized she'd been hit, and she teetered between anger and fear.

The dark vehicle was still on her left. She could just make it out in the rain. It was crowding her, bumping her, deliberately forcing her closer to the shoulder of the road. Paula gunned the engine, lurching forward, thinking she could get away, but she was coming up on a blind curve and she had to ease off the accelerator.

She frowned, puzzled, as the bigger car seemed to fall back just a little bit, and she felt her body go slack with relief as the distance between them increased.

But in the next instant the headlights bore down. She gasped, bracing for the impact. And then she was airborne, careening off into the blackness, and her scream died in her throat.

CHAPTER
~17~

The first thing Paula saw when she fought her way up from the cotton batting of oblivion was the familiar, pleated peach-colored shade of the lamp beside the bed in Belinda's guest room.

The second was the pinched little gamine face regarding her through enormous, azure eyes.

"Daddy!"

Lissa's screech seemed to enter Paula's brain and bounce off the edges of her consciousness.

"Daddy, it's Paula! Come here, Daddy! She's waking up! She's waking up!"

Making an effort to rouse herself, Paula felt her head begin to spin, and she lay back, grateful for the pillow, and tried to find her voice. "It's—all right, Lissa," she managed. "I'm fine. I'm going to be fine."

Before the child could answer, the door swung open and Ted loomed above the bed. He watched her for a moment, his handsome face a pastiche of emotions Paula could not identify. "Hey, there," he said, his voice strained. "At last. . . . Good morning, sleepyhead."

In a flash, before she could begin to wonder what she was doing in Belinda's guest room, it came flooding back. That dark-colored car. The rain-slick highway. The collision. The god-awful, sickening, helpless feeling that she was flying off into nothingness.

Blinking, she tried to conjure up a smile—primarily for Lissa's benefit. The poor baby was watching her, frightened, as though Paula might slip out of sight before her very eyes. But the simple effort to rearrange her face sent waves of pain through Paula's head, and when she tried to raise her right hand, she was startled to realize that her arm seemed to be encased in cement.

"Your arm's in a cast." Ted's smile was rueful. "Your left foot, too—although the cast may come off if the doctors decide that surgery's a better bet for your ankle."

Paula blinked again.

"You had a little accident."

She stared at him.

Ted sighed. "But you're all right. The highway patrolman said you're very lucky. It . . . could have been a lot worse."

Another piece of the memory surfaced. The officer leaning over her, shielding her face from the rain with his hat, talking gently as she shivered in the cold.

She remembered the smooth, white sheets on the gurney, the bumpy ride, the sirens, the flash of lights, the pain, the succession of bobbing, moving faces. And finally the blackness, a welcoming blackness that shut out the pain at last—and kept her from having to wrestle with herself when the patrol-man asked her questions.

Oh, yes, the questions.

"Did your car spin out?"

"Yes . . . yes, I guess so. . . ."

"Did something cause you to lose control of the wheel or was there another car involved?"

". . . There was . . . another car. . . ."

"Can you describe it? Did you happen to see a license number?"

Paula sighed, remembering the questions, re-membering the dilemma she'd faced. A dark-colored car with tinted windows had forced her off the road deliberately and with malice aforethought. Who had been driving it? The same person who'd warned her to stay away from Seaview? The same person who'd ravaged her mailbox looking for a letter from Belinda?

Ted? She groaned. Wynn Davidson? Had one of them killed Belinda? Was one of them determined to kill Paula, too, fearing she might know too much?

". . . lucky," Ted was saying. "There's a card in your wallet. Who to call in case of emergency. Belinda's name is on it. They called here from the emergency room at Seaview Hospital. . . ."

Paula looked down at the cast on her arm. At least it was her right arm. If it had been her left, she would have been more out of commission than she could even bear to think about.

Lissa was tugging at her other arm. "Paula, you slept for so long!"

"Did I, honey?" She turned to Ted. "How long *have* I been out?"

Ted shrugged. "It's Tuesday morning. The accident happened Sunday night. They released you from the hospital yesterday afternoon. We brought you here, and you've been sleeping ever since. But don't worry. I called your station manager."

Paula closed her eyes a moment. She did not remember coming back here. She supposed she'd been medicated, but it worried her anyway. She turned toward Lissa's pale little face. She tried another smile and was gratified to find she could manage it without as much pain. "Well, I guess I know why I'm feeling better. I have the world's best little nurse."

The child's face brightened. "Really, Paula? Can I be like a real nurse? Can I?"

"Of course, you can. You already are. I feel better just knowing you're here."

Lissa smiled. "See, Daddy? I told you I wouldn't be in the way. I was very, very quiet."

Ted cleared his throat. "Well. How about some soup, Paula? Surely you must be hungry."

She was. She nodded. "Sounds good, thanks." She watched him leave the room.

In summer the hills south of Mendocino would be dried yellow hulks, but now they were swollen by the winter rains, lush and silky and green.

Mike reached into a plastic bag tucked into a wedge between the bucket seats and plucked out another of Lou Schwartz's oatmeal raisin cookies. Then he settled back contentedly against the tan leather and munched as the landscape rolled by.

"Now you know why I'm thirty pounds over-weight," Celia murmured from the driver's seat. "There oughtta be a law against men who cook but never gain an ounce."

"It'll all catch up to him, mark my words." Mike

brushed crumbs from his lap. "He'll wake up one morning and, lo and behold, he'll weigh three hundred thirty pounds."

Celia shook her head. "Never happen. It's one of God's little ha-has. Men get character lines, and silver gray hair. Women get wrinkles and fat. And speaking of character lines, you're not getting any younger. Still no wedding bells in your future?"

Mike grinned. "You'll be the first to know."

"Good. I'll make you a shower."

They were nearly past it before they saw the sign, a rusting yellow square in a wrought-iron frame: *Martino Vineyards. Visitors Welcome.*

Celia made a sharp right onto a rutted, dirt road lined on both sides by gnarled grapevines that were totally devoid of foliage. Where the road ended, a Ford pickup that had once been green stood in front of a weathered, clapboard house.

At the sound of their car doors slamming shut, a man appeared on the porch, a wiry little guy with a furrowed, tanned face under a yellow straw hat.

"Mornin'." The furrowed face contorted into a smile. "Welcome to Martino Vineyards. Finest wines in Mendocino. You folks in the market?"

"Uh, not exactly." Mike stuck out a hand. "Mike Shaffer. Looking for Martin Gentry."

The smile faded. "Yeah? What for?"

"Are you Mr. Gentry?"

The eyes narrowed. "Maybe, maybe not. What is it you're after?"

"Information, mostly. I'm a lawyer, Mr. Gentry. I'm here about your nephew, Danny. This is Celia Schwartz. She's working with Danny, too. He's . . . in a little trouble down in Seaview."

The furrowed face settled into a scowl. "Yeah? Well, whadja come here for?"

"Because as far as we know, you're his only relative. He left White Rock to come and live with you."

"Pshh." It was a cross between a bleat and an expletive. "Well, he left. And I got nothin' to say."

Mike listened to the drone of a helicopter and considered how he might change Gentry's mind. But before he could formulate anything that seemed vaguely reasonable, Celia came forward, smiling.

"What kind of grapes do you grow, Mr. Gentry?" The smile would have dazzled a sultan, and she waved her left hand in such a way that her diamond ring sparked fire in the sunlight. "It must be terribly gratifying to produce your own wine. I said that to my husband the other day. . . ."

She was talking to Zach when Ted knocked on the door. "Paula, there's a highway patrolman here to see you."

She hesitated, juggling the receiver. "I'm on the phone, Ted. Tell him I'll be right with him." She spoke into the phone. "Listen, Zach, I just can't go on camera trussed up like a turkey at Christmastime. I'll call you tomorrow after I see the doctor and I have some idea what's going on—"

There was another rap on the door, and an officer in crisp khaki stepped into the room. He was holding his cap, and he looked huge and uncomfortable against the ruffles in Belinda's guest room.

"Zach, a CHP officer's here to see me. I really have to go. The station will live without me for a few days. I'll call you tomorrow, I promise." She hung up and, with her left hand gestured to the peach-colored chair. "I'm sorry, Officer—"

"Chandler."

"Please sit down. Sorry. I guess I should have come to see you."

"No problem." Chandler tried to look efficient and professional, but his face relaxed into a sheepish grin. "I just—while you were talking just now, I realized who you are. I mean I knew the name and all, but when you said something about the station, I realized. You're on KSFO."

Paula smiled. "That's a long way from Seaview. Do you spend much time in the Bay area?"

Chandler shook his head. "Not too much time, no. But occasionally. I've seen your show. You're good."

"Well, thank you." Clearly the man was interested, but she decided not to encourage him. She kept her voice businesslike. "Anything new on the car that ran me off the road?"

"Uh, right." He shifted a little in his seat. "Of course. That's why I came here. You told the officer who was with you that night that you thought the car that hit you was black."

"Pretty sure, yes. I think it was black. I know it had dark, tinted windows."

"Could the car have been blue? We found a blue Toyota Celica abandoned off the highway next morning. It had a dented right front fender. No paint on it that matched your car, but we thought—"

"It could have been dark blue, but it wasn't a Celica," Paula said. "The car that hit me was big. It was a big, solid, American-made car, like a Bonneville or a Coupe de Ville. It was definitely not a Celica."

"Yes, ma'am." Chandler nodded. "Well, do you think it's possible the driver didn't know he'd hit you?"

Paula shook her head. "It is not possible, Officer Chandler. The driver knew exactly what he was doing. He bumped me once or twice before he hit. He forced me toward the right shoulder of the road and then he hit me hard."

"You believe it was a deliberate hit and run."

"Very deliberate. Yes."

"Ms. Carroll, you told us you'd left Seaview maybe twenty minutes before the accident. Were you followed onto the highway? Were you aware of the presence of this other car behind you on the road?"

She shook her head again. "I was not aware of it. If it followed me onto the highway, I didn't know it. I became aware of it when it bumped me the first time. It took me completely by surprise."

Chandler looked at her, and she knew what was coming even before the words were out: "Then I have to ask you this, Ms. Carroll. Do you know of anyone who wants to harm you?"

Well, yes, she could say. *I'm beginning to think it was my best friend's husband. The man who let you in downstairs. See, he murdered his wife when she found out he's responsible for exposing their little girl to contaminants, and he trashed my mailbox to keep me from finding out, but I did find out, and now he wants to kill me. . . .*

Chandler waited, and Paula looked away, knowing how foolish that would sound.

Or how about, *Yes, a man named Wynn Davidson. His company is responsible for the contamination. He killed Belinda because she threatened to let me in on it, so now, of course, he wants to kill me, too. . . .*

The officer waited. He cleared his throat.

"No, Officer Chandler. I don't."

CHAPTER

~18~

Celia had barely backed out of the rutted driveway and turned onto the main road when Mike began to snicker.

"That was," he said, "without any doubt, the most underhanded, unprofessional behavior it has ever been my pleasure to witness."

Celia shrugged, turning to wink at him. "I know. Worked, didn't it?"

"Oh, sure." Mike took on a wounded tone. "Just don't ask me what I would have done if you'd whipped out your checkbook and made Gentry an offer on the whole sorry little vineyard."

"No chance." Celia laughed her deep, hearty laugh. "Cheap wine gives me a headache. And anyway, the guy was too eager. But what the heck, it got him talking."

It had indeed, Mike reflected, reviewing what Gentry had told them—valuable information that not only filled in some blanks but shored up the case for his defense of Danny as a gentle, harmless soul.

Celia must have been thinking the same thing. Her voice was uncustomarily sad. "So damned easy for most people to have children. Too bad they don't have to take lessons on how not to screw 'em up. . . ."

Danny had been born twenty years ago, Gentry'd told them, to Martin's sister, Felicia Marie Gentry. She'd been fourteen years old and seven moths along before anyone knew she was pregnant, and by the time she was eighteen, she knew one thing: She had no taste for motherhood—especially for mothering a big hulk of a kid who, it had become pretty obvious, was not quite right in the head.

The story'd made a splash in the local paper when the child had been abandoned in a parking lot. But, Martin Gentry whined, he'd been in no position to offer the boy a home.

"I figgered," he'd said, his lower lip trembling, "that little Danny'd be better fed by the county than anything I could manage."

But, he'd droned on, he felt more and more guilty as the years went rolling by. "I knew I owed that boy a home," he said. "The home my shiftless sister never made for him."

Of course, the fact that Gentry had inherited the winery three years ago—all to himself, since Felicia had never been heard from again since the day she'd disappeared—had nothing at all to do with his decision. It wasn't that Gentry needed a hand on the land—oh, no, nothing like that! It was just that he couldn't sleep nights anymore for his guilt. So he traced Danny to White Rock Academy and "paid the boy a little visit."

"You know," Celia said, "if there'd just been the winery, Danny might be there still. From what that

Tulley fellow told you at White Rock Academy,
Danny liked to work the earth. . . ."

But Gentry had also raised chickens for a while
and slaughtered them for a butcher shop in Mendocino. And Danny "had fits—just came unglued—
every time it came time for the slaughterin'."

So it had not surprised Gentry to wake up one
morning and find that Danny had gone. "Took everything with him that wasn't tied down, that's the
gratitude he repaid me with. But that's okay, the
Lord Himself knows I did my level best."

Celia pulled off the road into a gravel parking
area. "How about some lunch?" she asked.

Mike looked skeptically at the handpainted signs.
Hansen Farms Market. But Celia had already
parked in the shade of an olive tree and was getting
out of the car.

"Trust me," she called back over her shoulder.
"They'll have fabulous bread and cheese. And, anyway, if I bring Lou some vine-ripened olives, he'll be
my sex slave for a week!"

"I saw a real bride once," Lissa piped, carefully
unfolding the layers of tissue packed around Belinda's bride doll. "Amy-who-used-to-babysit-me got to
be a bride, and she let me see her in her bride's
dress."

"I'll bet she was beautiful," Paula leaned back
against the pillows and marveled at the dexterity of
Lissa's chubby little fingers.

"Ye-es." Lissa shrugged, pouting a little as she
lifted the doll from its swaddling. "But she wasn't as
pretty as Mommy, I bet. Mommy was the prettiest
bride."

Paula gazed at the porcelain features of the doll

Lissa was holding. On the one hand, she was glad that Lissa could talk about Belinda without bursting into tears. It must mean that her sessions with Dr. Irvin had to be helping her to cope. On the other hand, she felt a stab of fresh pain remembering her friend's wedding day. Without doubt, Belinda had been one of the loveliest brides she had ever seen.

Ted had just accepted a promotion at the state's safety office in San Diego, and because he was to begin a scant week after Belinda's graduation, he and Belinda had decided to move the wedding up to the week before final exams so that they would have time for a honeymoon.

It was a crazy week, what with dress fittings and wedding rehearsals jammed in between cramming for finals, and on the day of the wedding the cake had not arrived less than half an hour before the ceremony. But Belinda, standing in the church vestry, remained a perfect oasis of calm.

"Nothing can happen until I'm ready," she'd told Paula as she adjusted the folds of her veil. *"If the cake isn't here, I just won't step outside. They won't start the wedding march without me."*

Paula, stiff and nervous in the aquamarine satin of her maid of honor's dress, had looked at Belinda with wonder. For the first time she was forced to realize that maybe, after all, Belinda would manage without her help—even in San Diego, half a state away from where Paula would be working in Ventura.

"Belinda," she'd whispered, missing her already, *"promise me you're going to look after yourself. You'll have your college degree, too, you know. You'll find yourself a wonderful job—and we'll call each other every Sunday. We'll always be in touch."*

It was weeks until that harrowing night before their graduation—weeks before they made the pact that would bind their lives together. And yet Paula had known, even then, that Belinda would always be a part of her—her alter ego, no matter the miles that marked the distance between them.

"Paula." Lissa was tugging at her arm. "Can we comb the dolly's hair?"

Blinking, Paula looked down at the doll and removed the little wedding veil. Then she took the hairbrush Lissa handed her and began to sweep the doll's dark hair back, pinning it up into a cascade of curls the way Belinda had worn hers on her wedding day.

But separate they had, she recalled wistfully, Belinda to San Diego with Ted, and Paula to the little coastal town of Ventura and the beginning of her broadcasting career.

Remembering those early days at KVKW, Paula thought about Todd Hazeltine and the phone conversation she'd had with him less than a week ago.

It had indeed been Ted Raymond who had inspected the refinery site in Seaview. It had been Ted who'd finally issued the order of "imminent and/or substantial public endangerment," mandating the state to declare the refinery's owners responsible for cleaning up the pollution.

But a long period of time had elapsed since the city's initial requests for help, time the refinery owners—Duncan Associates—had used to their advantage.

During that time Duncan Associates had filed for the protection of bankruptcy, maintaining that the company was some ten million dollars in debt, and the court had allowed them to abandon their interest in the refinery since they could not come up with the forty million it would take to clean up the environmental mess. All of which meant that innocent children would continue to be exposed to the pollution until the state either waged an uphill battle with the courts or bit the bullet and cleaned it up itself.

Paula could imagine Belinda's rage at learning of the awful contamination. Had she understood that her husband's footdragging had allowed Duncan Associates to declare bankruptcy? More than that, had she known about—or suspected—a connection between Ted and Duncan Associates?

Was that why she'd written that letter to Wynn Davidson? Was that why she was dead? And was that why Paula had been run off the road, lucky not to have met her end in what could have been a fatal crash?

Paula had been *lucky,* Ted had told her. Her injuries were relatively minor. *Was* she lucky—or were Ted's very words hiding an implicit threat?

"Paula!" Lissa's voice was demanding. Paula fought off the reverie and forced herself to concentrate on adjusting the doll's headpiece and arranging the little bridal veil just so.

Wynn Davidson's phone number—the number Sam had given her—was tucked away in her purse. She had not called him because she was still debating the advisability of the call. After all, Belinda had used Paula as a warning of sorts to Davidson, and the likelihood that he would talk to her under those circumstances seemed a little slim. What made more sense, it seemed to her, was to investigate the current status of Duncan Associates. And given

Paula's "accident," it could be increasingly dangerous for her to investigate at all. . . .

"Hall-ooo!"

The cheery voice made Paula jump, but Lissa
stood up and smiled. "It's Mrs. Morrissey!" She ran
to the head of the stairs. "We're up here, in the guest
room! Me and Paula are playing bride dolls. Do you
want to come up and play?"

"Hi, sweetie." The voice grew closer as Judy Morrissey climbed the stairs. "I brought over a casserole
for your dinner—Oh, my goodness, look at that! It's
the prettiest bride doll I've ever seen!"

Paula, glad for the adult company, was neverthe-
less dismayed. The front door should have been
locked. Anyone could have walked in. "Hi," she said,
mustering a smile. "The doll belonged to Belinda.
Lissa managed to retrieve it somehow when Ted had
the Salvation Army folks come in and clean out all
Belinda's closets."

Judy pressed her lips together. "I know. It seemed
awfully fast. I offered to help Ted go through her
things, but he told me he'd already had it done. . . ."

Paula glanced at Lissa, who was arranging the
petticoats under the doll's little satin wedding gown.
"Lissa, honey, would you be a good girl and run down
and lock the front door? And maybe, while you're
down there, you could find us some cookies. I'll bet
Mrs. Morrissey would like that."

Lissa didn't need to be asked a second time. She
grinned and put the doll down on Paula's bed. They
heard her singing as she skipped down the stairs.
"Cook-kies for the wedd-ding!"

Judy Morrissey gave Paula a thumbs up sign.
"Seems like she's doing pretty well."

"I think so." Paula nodded.

Judy smiled. "Thank heaven for the resiliency of children. . . ."

"Judy . . ." Paula hesitated, though she wanted to ask the question before Lissa came skipping back. "You know about the pollution at the old refinery?"

Judy nodded. "Yes, of course."

"Belinda was very bothered by it, wasn't she?"

"Oh, yes! It was she who organized the meetings, got the parents together . . . although . . . toward the last . . . I don't know . . . she seemed to be losing her enthusiasm. . . ."

Losing her enthusiasm. . . . Paula wondered. Had Belinda learned how deeply Ted was involved? Did she suspect, toward the last, that because of Ted's complicity, it might be months—maybe even years—before the contamination would be cleaned up? Or perhaps she had been upset because her husband's complicity was apt to be made public.

"Is something wrong?" Paula had asked her.

". . . Yes. I guess you could say that."

"Between you and Ted?"

". . . Well—yes. . . ."

She hadn't wanted to discuss it on the phone, and if she'd put her concerns in a letter to Paula, it had been stolen from a smashed mailbox. . . .

"Judy,"—Paula spoke quickly, knowing Lissa would be back any minute—"Belinda kept a daily diary. She had several years' worth in her closet. I saw them. But they must have gone to the Salvation Army Thrift Shop along with the rest of her things. Do you suppose—I mean, I can't think anyone would want them. The people at the thrift store may have thrown them out. But—just in case—would you mind checking? See if maybe they're still packed in some box?"

"We have some Nutter Butters!" Lissa announced, her gaze fastened on the plate she was carrying.

"I've got to get home," Judy Morrissey said, looking down at her watch. "But—sure. If you think it's important, Paula, I'll check at the thrift store tomorrow."

CHAPTER

— 19 —

The good news, the doctor told Paula on Wednesday, was that the broken metatarsals in her left foot appeared to be mending nicely. The bad news was, she'd find it difficult—maybe even impossible—to get around with any competence on crutches while her right arm was in a cast.

But the cast would have to remain on her arm for a while longer, and Paula, hating the helplessness of the wheelchair, insisted on getting the crutches. Despite the fact that she was enjoying her time with Lissa, she had neither the time nor the patience to be an invalid in Ted's house.

"Take it easy, Paula," Ted snapped, helping her from the wheelchair into the car. "Bones take their time to heal, and you can't speed up the process just because you want to."

No, Paula thought, pressing her lips together, *but I won't be dependent on you.*

Ted seemed to vacillate these days between tense silence and nervous energy. She'd hated to depend on him even to get her to the doctor this morning. There had been no choice, but now she was anxious to get to the house and let him get back to work. From a chair in the kitchen, she could supervise the lunch-making. Lissa, who seemed to be enjoying "taking care" of Paula, could certainly manage sandwiches.

Settled in the car at last, the newly rented aluminum crutches stretched across the backseat, Paula stared straight ahead into the sunny day and wondered whether the best tack to take with Ted was one of confrontation, solicitude, or simple, innocent curiosity.

The decision was taken out of her hands. Ted glanced at her as he drove. "I apologize if I've been short with you, Paula—or with Lissa, for that matter. I've . . . been under a lot of strain these past days. And you're very distant. Cold, almost. Not at all like your usual self."

"Sorry," she murmured, kicking herself for allowing him to pick up the change in her attitude. The last thing she wanted to do was alert him to what she was thinking. "You have to realize this is difficult for me, too. And I'm worried about getting back to my job."

To some extent, the latter was true. She needed to get back to San Francisco. There was a limit to how long the station could do without her and, as Zach had casually reminded her, how long Stu Snyder would wait.

Funny how the idea of anchoring a network news show—once the most important goal of her life—could suddenly seem so trivial. . . .

When Mike was a kid, he'd had a babysitter, a pretty, red-haired girl with long, thick braids who played the piano exquisitely. She could sit on that piano bench in the Shaffers' living room and make the old upright sing.

But she only did it when nobody was listening—or when she thought nobody was. If little Mike got out of bed and wandered out for a drink, she would stop playing, clamp her lips together, and close the lid over the keyboard.

Mike thought of that now, as he walked toward the visiting room of the Seaview Jail and listened to the silvery tones coming from Danny's harmonica.

He was glad he'd made the trip to Mendocino with Celia, less because of what he'd learned than because of what he'd confirmed: Danny Gentry was not a killer. Violence was not in his nature—not against animals, not against people—almost certainly not against a gentle woman he considered to be his friend.

What was he doing in Belinda's kitchen that evening, clutching the bloody knife in his hand? Who had been there before Danny got there—and maybe convinced the boy he had killed her?

The melody Danny was playing was not one Mike recognized, but it was sweet and plaintive, hauntingly familiar—a little like "Scarlet Ribbons." Danny waved when he saw Mike, but he played to the end of the piece. When he stopped, he wiped the harmonica carefully with his shirttail before he put it back in his pocket.

"That was beautiful, Danny," Mike told him truthfully. "You have a gift for music, do you know that?"

Danny shrugged the way a child would, his large head resting on his shoulder. He looked pleased, but he said nothing. He just watched Mike.

"I saw your uncle yesterday, Danny." Mike pulled

up a chair and sat. "You remember your uncle Martin, don't you? And the winery in Mendocino?"

Danny shrugged again, less deeply this time. "Chickens. Martin has chickens." His brown eyes darkened. "Danny likes the chickens, but Martin don't. Martin want to cut off their heads."

"And Danny didn't like that."

Danny shook his head. "Danny goes away."

Mike paused. The words were primitive, but the ideas came through loud and clear. It was the most lucid conversation he'd had with Danny. He decided to press his luck. "So you went away, and you came to Seaview. And there you met Belinda. Where did you meet Belinda, Danny? How did she come to be your frie—"

Danny rose from his chair with such force that it skidded back and fell over. "Belinda dead! Danny did it. Lot of blood, more than the chickens."

"A lot of blood. Where was the blood?"

"All over. Blood all over."

Mike took the chance. "The blood came from knife wounds, Danny. Did you put the knife in Belinda?"

Danny shook his head, his dark eyes terrified.

"You didn't put the knife in, did you?"

Danny hesitated. He looked confused. Mike made the educated guess. "Did you see the blood when you came in the kitchen? Did you see the knife in Belinda?"

Danny wailed. He began to sway. "Knife. Knife in Belinda."

"What did you do?"

Danny sank to his knees. "Danny bend down. Bend down. Belinda look at Danny. 'Oh, God,' she says. 'Danny. Oh, God, Danny . . .'"

Mike felt his own heart pounding. "Then what did you do?"

Danny cried softly. "Danny take out knife. More blood. Belinda's eyes close. . . ."

"Danny take out knife. . . ."

All at once the kid seemed to cave in on himself. He lay in a heap, his body trembling. Mike waited until the sobs subsided. Then he laid a hand on Danny's shoulder. "Danny," he said. "You didn't kill Belinda. Not if the knife was in her when you got there."

Danny looked up, his face streaked, his large dark eyes luminous. "I killed her. Belinda's eyes open. I take out knife. Eyes close."

Mike shook his head. "No, Danny. You tried to help her. You took out the knife because you knew she was hurt. You were Belinda's friend. But it was too late for you to help her. She was already hurt too badly."

"Hurt . . ." Danny blinked, but tears filled his eyes. "Hurt. Who hurt Belinda?"

Mike patted Danny's shoulder. "I don't know. But we're going to find out."

Lissa had managed bologna sandwiches just fine and had even, much to Paula's surprise, agreed that a nap was a good idea. She had climbed the stairs like a little trooper and closed her bedroom door behind her.

Paula planned to call the station and bring them up to date on her condition. Crutches or no, she would be ready for the cameras as soon as the bruises faded, even if it meant she would have to hire someone at home to help her get dressed and get around.

Lissa had brought her some magazines to read, but Paula had other ideas. She reached for one crutch and slid forward in her chair. Moving awkwardly, she leaned forward and put her weight on her right foot, then used her right arm and the weight of the cast to push herself up from the chair.

Wobbly, but feeling a heady sense of power, she propelled herself forward a few steps. When the doorbell rang, she felt more awkward than she'd ever felt in her life. "Who is it?" she called.

"Paula? It's me, Sam!"

Absurdly happy to hear his voice, she hobbled to the front door and managed, somehow, with her left hand, to turn the latch on the lock.

Sam stood in the doorway for a long moment, his expression changing from joy to distress. Then he folded her to him, and she felt herself relax for the first time in days.

"I was in Los Angeles," he whispered into her hair. "I just got back this morning. I called Ted to see how things were going and he told me—Paula, are you all right?"

She nodded as he helped her into the living room and settled her on the sofa. "A few bruises, a few broken bones. As Ted says, it could have been worse. Somebody forced me off the road. It could have been a lot worse."

Sam's expression changed from concern to anger. "Have they found the bastard who hit you?"

She shook her head.

"Well, why the hell not? Who's on it, the CHP?"

Paula nodded. "I'm sure they're doing everything they can. It was raining. I didn't get a license number—"

"I don't care. I've got friends in the department.

Let me see what I can find out." He sat next to her and took her hands in his. "Thank God you're all right."

The irony of it struck her as hilarious. *Thank God you're all right.* And there she was, trussed up in two casts with purple bruises all over her!

Before she could stop it, the laughter bubbled up and she found herself beginning to giggle, and then she was laughing not only at the circumstances, but at the horrified expression on Sam's face.

As usual, he seemed to read her mind and understand why she was laughing, and he joined in and the two of them laughed until they doubled over and their sides hurt.

Sam was the first to catch his breath. "Oh, Lord"—he wiped a tear from his eye—"I don't remember the last time I laughed that hard. God, but it felt good."

Paula nodded, leaning back in her seat. "It's truly amazing, isn't it? The human need to find itself some solace, even in the midst of pain. . . ."

Sam's expression turned sober. "How I miss her. Belinda, I mean. I really do. A simple thing like this trip to L.A., and so many little things fell apart—the kinds of things Belinda would have nailed tight. There'll never be anybody like her. . . ."

Paula closed her eyes. "She loved it, you know. She loved working for you. She was always telling me how brilliant you are, how organized, how detail-oriented."

"I wish." He smiled ruefully. "The truth is, I'm only smart enough to surround myself with bright people. Belinda not only knew what she was doing, she could charm the skin off a snake! . . . I remember one time—in Los Angeles, as a matter of fact—we were entertaining a group of Japanese businessmen who were thinking of investing in our Tartan Companies. Belinda took the whole lot of non-English speaking wives on a tour of the Los Angeles County Museum of Art, then got them settled happily back at their hotel in time to dress to the nines and have dinner with me and the grateful husbands."

Paula looked at him. "She acted as your hostess?"

"Oh, many times, yes. There is no Mrs. Pierce, as you know. Belinda didn't mind. She seemed to enjoy hostessing. She'd travel with me whenever I needed her."

Paula thought a minute. *"Belinda didn't mind. Belinda seemed to enjoy hostessing."* She was sure that was true. But a new thought surfaced. Maybe Ted *had* minded. She found herself turning to Sam. "Sam, you're aware that Belinda was distressed over the environmental hazards at the refinery."

"Well, yes—"

"Among other things, she had organized a parents' group to put pressure on the owners to clean it up."

Sam nodded. "Yes, I think she mentioned that, but—"

"Did she ever mention that Ted might have been . . . involved in a ruse to delay the cleanup?"

Sam paused. "Ted? I don't think so."

"Well, I think he was involved up to his teeth, and I think Belinda knew it." Paula sat up straighter. "Do you remember when I asked you about Duncan Associates? About a man named Wynn Davidson?"

"Of course."

"Well, I think possibly there's some kind of relationship between Ted and this Wynn Davidson. Ted did the site inspection that finally led to the refinery's being named a public danger. But he dragged his feet on the inspection so long that Davidson's company had time enough to declare bankruptcy and wiggle out of its fiscal responsibility to clean the area up."

Sam frowned. "Why would he do that?"

"I don't know. . . ." But she found herself thinking.

An image of the gowns she had seen in Belinda's closet floated into her consciousness. Beautiful gowns that Sam had bought for her. How had Ted felt about that?

Was he jealous when he saw her in those lovely gowns? Upset that he couldn't afford to buy them? Upset enough to accept a "gift" from Davidson in return for dragging his feet?

On the one hand, it seemed farfetched. On the other, it made extraordinary sense. . . . What if Belinda had found out what Ted had done? What might she have decided to do about it? And how threatened—how angry might that have made Ted?

"Sam," she began, grateful for the sounding board on which to try out her theory.

CHAPTER

~20~

"Hey, counselor," Dickie Hetherington called. "Gotta minute for an old buddy?"

Mike Shaffer, heading toward the exit of the jail, didn't seem to hear him. Dickie whistled through his teeth, and Mike turned around.

His old high school classmate was spending a lot of time with this homeless suspect, Dickie thought. According to the logbook, Mike had been in to see the Gentry kid at all sorts of odd hours.

Dickie gestured Mike over, then sat down and hooked a leg over his chair. Not that it was any of *his* business how Mike Shaffer worked. But he had to admit he was plenty curious if it had anything to do with Paula Carroll. And anyway it was always fun to drop a piece of official gossip to a friend.

"Hey, man"—he took a swig of muddy-tasting coffee—"been over to see Paula Carroll?"

Mike blinked. "Paula? No. As far as I know she's in San Francisco."

Dickie shook his head. "Nosirree. She's at the

Raymond house recuperating from an accident. I just happened to be playing poker last night with Hank Chandler. He's a Chippie, you know. California Highway Patrol? Seems Paula sailed off the shoulder of the highway the other night. Seems she may have had a little help."

"What does that mean?"

Dickie shrugged. "She said she was run off the road."

Mike took a moment to digest the information and quell a stab of alarm in his gut. "Is she okay?"

"Broken arm, broken foot. Chandler said she was lucky."

Mike nodded. "Lucky. Yeah, right. . . . Well, thanks for the tip." He raised a hand in a gesture of salute and headed out the door.

It had rained earlier, but now the sun was strong and steam seemed to curl up from the sidewalks. Humidity was unusual as far north as Seaview, but this seemed to be an unusually warm winter, and Mike's shirt was sticking to his back before he got to his office building.

Two things rattled around in his brain as he loosened his tie and trudged up the stairs. One was that he was far too personally upset when he'd found out Paula had been hurt.

The other was that if, as Dickie had suggested, her accident was not really an accident, then it could have implications beyond the obvious . . . implications that could be helpful to his client.

He was halfway up the stairs when he turned around, drummed his fingernails against the banister for a second, then picked up his pace, straightened up his tie, and made a beeline for his car.

"I'm really sorry, Paula." Judy Morrissey handed her a small address book bound in blue flowered cloth. "I went through everything with a thrift shop volunteer, but this was all we could find among . . . her things."

Paula looked down at the little book and flipped haphazardly through its pages. Business and personal addresses were entered alphabetically in Belinda's neat script. Here and there were notes in the margin in a curious sort of shorthand.

Judy had brought her daughter home from preschool with Lissa, and the two little girls were watching them. It didn't seem the right time to ask questions.

"Well," she said, making her way awkwardly to a kitchen shelf filled with cookbooks. She tucked the little volume in among them. "Thanks for trying, anyway, Judy. . . . Would you and Tiffany like to stay for something to eat?"

Judy looked doubtful, but the girls joined hands and began to jump up and down. "Ye-ess!"

"Okay, okay," Judy relented. "But then Paula will need to rest. You girls can gather up your skates, and I'll take you both to the park."

They fixed a light lunch of cheese *quesadillas* and a salad of sliced tomatoes and cucumbers, and the girls took their plates out to the patio, leaving Paula and Judy in the kitchen.

"Paula," Judy began in that thoughtful tone people always use when they are going to ask a favor.

Paula waited, and Judy didn't disappoint her. "I hope this isn't presumptuous of me . . . but I have some friends—people I used to teach with—who are trying to get a cable television station in place. It would be housed right here at Seaview Junior College, but it would serve a fairly wide area."

"Sounds great." Paula knew there was more.

"They already have funding," Judy said. "What they need is know-how. Experienced know-how. They're looking for an executive producer. . . ."

Paula frowned. "An executive producer. . . . Well, I'll be happy to pass the word."

"Well, actually"—Judy went on in a rush—"they were thinking about somebody like you. I mean, I mentioned you, and they seemed to think it was a wonderful idea, and . . . well, I wondered if you'd mind if they called you."

The prospect was intriguing if a little farfetched. She'd never done any producing. But there was nothing to be lost by hearing the pitch. "Sure." She shrugged. "Anytime."

Peals of laughter came from the patio. It gave Paula a warm feeling.

"Lissa is lucky to have Tiffany," she said, looking out at the girls.

"It works both ways," Judy assured her. "Lissa is a terrific little kid."

"She is, isn't she?" Paula couldn't help the surge of pride she felt. "I'll worry about her when I go back to the city and she's left here alone with Ted."

Judy looked at her oddly. "Oh, Ted's a good father. Really! He's wonderful with Lissa."

"Well, yes, of course, he is! It isn't that," Paula told her quickly. What was it she'd been thinking, exactly? That a little girl needs a mother? Or that a man who might be capable of murdering his wife. . . . The doorbell cut into her thoughts.

• • •

Mike recognized the woman who answered the door. She'd been taking the little girl—Lissa was her name—off somewhere or other the last time he'd come to see Paula. "Mike Shaffer," he told her by way of introduction. "I'd like to see Paula if she's here."

The woman seemed to recognize him, too. "Hello. I'm Judy Morrissey. If you'll wait a second, I'll tell her you're here. We were just about to leave."

Through the partially opened door, he could hear her talking to Paula, calling, "Girls, finish up. It's time to go!"

After a long moment Paula came to the door, leaning heavily on one crutch. She wore two plaster casts and she looked paler than he remembered, and when she looked up at him, he saw a yellowish purple bruise running down her cheek and across her neck.

"Mr. Shaffer."

"Mike."

"Mike, of course."

He couldn't quite read the expression on her face. But she stepped back as though to let him in, and he didn't need a second invitation. She didn't resist when he gave her his arm to lean on and helped her to the sofa in the living room.

Judy Morrissey appeared in the doorway with two little girls in tow. One he recognized as Lissa. She gave him a smile and a wave.

"We're going skating."

"Well, that sounds like fun."

Judy stepped forward. "Anything you need before we leave, Paula?"

"Thanks, Judy. No. I'll be fine."

"Okay. Well, I guess we'll be going then. We'll be back in plenty of time for supper."

Mike stood awkwardly until they'd gone, then he sat in the chair Paula indicated. "I . . . just heard. About your accident and all. I hope you don't mind my coming by."

A slight hesitation. "This a social call then."

"Uh, partially, yes."

"Partially. I see. Well, and the other part? Was there something else you wanted?"

He decided to stop beating around the bush. "I was talking to a friend of mine at the Seaview police station. Apparently he has a friend on the CHP. That's how I found out about your . . . accident. And I wondered . . ." He hesitated, clearing his throat. "I wondered exactly what happened. I mean, I understand you said you'd been forced off the road. I wonder if you have any idea by whom."

She was bright, but then he knew that. He saw the hint of a smile cross her face. "And if I did," she began, "why would I tell you? Anything I told you might help you defend your client, whom the D.A. still believes killed Belinda."

Mike got up from his chair and began to pace, jamming his hands in his pockets. "Look," he said, "I have a file full of documents that tell the story of Danny Gentry. He's a nice kid, a gentle soul, not a violent bone in his body. Despite what you may believe, I think I have enough to convince a jury he did not kill Belinda Raymond. And while technically, that's where my job ends, I happen to care who *did* kill Belinda. I've known her since we were kids, you know. I'd give a lot to pinpoint her killer."

He saw Paula swallow hard. "Why are you telling me all this?"

"Because the first time I saw you here, you had a screaming fit when I even *mentioned* her husband as a possible suspect. But later, last Saturday when I met you at the ice cream shop, you seemed to have . . . mellowed a little. You talked about the refinery, and I wondered—I don't know. I guess I'm wondering what you *are* thinking."

If thoughts were choo-choo trains, Mike thought to himself, then Paula Carroll was the Orient Express, so quickly did ideas seem to flash across her face only to be replaced by new ones. Finally she seemed to come to a decision. She looked squarely at Mike.

"What I told you," she said, her voice well modulated, "was that Belinda was angry over the refinery site—that she was organizing a parents' group for the purpose of working toward getting the mess cleaned up."

Mike nodded. "That's what you told me."

She hesitated. "All right. But there's more. Belinda had traced the present ownership of the refinery to a company called Duncan Associates in Las Vegas—a corporation run by a man named Wynn Davidson. Ever hear of him?"

He shook his head.

"Well, it seems the company declared bankruptcy and managed to wiggle off the financial hook for the cleanup. Belinda had written Davidson a letter telling him, in effect, that he had the ethics of an alleycat—that his cavalier attitude was all the more monstrous because children were being exposed to his toxic nightmare."

Mike listened, knowing there was more. Paula seemed to take her time. Finally she drew a ragged breath. "Belinda also threatened to use her influence with me. She said she would ask me to denounce Davidson publicly, using my television news show as a forum. . . ."

Now the whole thing took on some relevance, though it seemed a little far-out to Mike. "Let me be sure I understand you," he said. "You're implying there's a very good possibility that Davidson took Belinda at her word—that he murdered her, or had her murdered, in order to shut her up—and further that you may have been run off the road because you were privy to what Belinda knew."

Paula nodded. "As a matter of fact, it was only recently that I learned what Belinda knew. But it's one theory, anyway. You asked me what I was thinking."

Mike took a deep breath and let the air out slowly. He ran a hand through his sandy-blond hair and sank into the chair across from Paula.

"You don't put much stock in it," Paula murmured.

"I didn't say that. I need to kick it around. About the only thing I feel certain about at this point is that Danny did not kill Belinda."

There was a moment's silence, a time when each of them seemed to be taking the other's measure. Finally it was he who broke the silence. "Listen," he said, "I need a favor. Don't ask me why and don't jump to conclusions. It's asking a lot, I know. But trust me if you possibly can. I need a picture of Ted Raymond."

She did not respond for a long time. She just sat there, staring at him. Then she gestured to a table near his chair. "In the drawer. I think there's a photo album."

He moved quickly, before she could change her mind, retrieved the album, and handed it to her. She flipped through the pages, removed a photo, and handed it to him without a word.

"Thank you," he told her, unreasonably happy that, in fact, she had chosen to trust him. He took the album from her lap and put it back in the drawer.

They both looked up at the sound of a car door. "Well," he said, "I guess I should be going."

Paula nodded.

"When do you get the casts off?"

"Soon, I hope. I have to get back to work."

"If there's anything I can do—"

She smiled. "I don't think so. But thanks—for the part of the visit that was social."

The door swung open and a man stepped in. He set his briefcase down and looked warily at the two of them.

"Ted, you're home early." Paula heaved herself up. "Mike, this is Ted Raymond." She turned, wobbling against her crutch. "Ted, this is Mike Shaffer."

There was a long pause as Ted Raymond struggled to put a meaning to the name. Then he must have remembered, because his face flushed dark red. "You're the scum who's defending that half-wit. You've got one hell of a nerve," he bellowed. "Get the hell out of my house!"

CHAPTER

~21~

Ted was furious. To his credit, he tried to act calm in front of Lissa, but dinner—a hastily thrown together spaghetti and meat sauce—was a strained and awkward affair, and afterward they could hear him in the kitchen, banging pots and pans with abandon. In all the years she'd known him, Paula could not remember seeing him quite so angry, and it made her wonder if Belinda had been subjected to the same kind of temper tantrums through the years.

His behavior seemed like an overreaction at the least. Paula could understand his being upset at finding Mike Shaffer in his living room. After all, Shaffer was defending the man who had allegedly killed Ted's wife. But if, as Ted maintained, he had nothing to hide, then what was the point of his fury? He had never even bothered to ask what Mike had been doing in the house in the first place.

Paula felt Lissa tugging at her sleeve. "Come *on*, Paula, it's your *turn!*"

She looked down at the Chutes and Ladders game

board as though she were seeing it for the first time. "Sorry." She smiled, picking up the dice and moving her yellow marker four spaces.

She did not believe she'd been disloyal to tell Mike Shaffer about Belinda's letter to Wynn Davidson. Ted knew how upset Belinda had been about the delay in cleaning up the refinery site. The only question in Paula's mind was whether she'd known what part Ted had played in that delay.

Still, in no way during her talk with Mike, had she implicated Ted at all—even though her own suspicions were moving swiftly in his direction. Although, of course, she had given Mike the photo. What did he want the photo for . . . ?

She looked up guiltily when she heard Ted's voice. He was standing directly in front of her at the dining room table. "Sorry," she heard herself apologizing, "I guess I didn't hear you."

He looked at her coldly. "I'm going out. If you need something, Lissa can help."

She nodded.

"I won't be long," he added lamely. "There's—something I have to do."

Lissa won two games in a row, but she was clearly bored with Chutes and Ladders. "Can we watch TV?" she asked Paula, tossing the pieces into the box. "I can help you get into the living room!"

Belinda had not allowed much television, but Lissa looked so earnest. And she hadn't watched any TV in the week that Paula had been there. It seemed like a passable idea.

The hamburger sizzling on the grill smelled wonderful. Mike hadn't realized he was so hungry. But by the time it had finished cooking and he'd piled salad on his plate, he could hardly wait to dig in.

Next to early morning, this was the time of day he most appreciated his deck overlooking the steep arroyo. The sun seemed to set just past the edge of his property line, turning the sky a dozen brilliant hues. He watched it change as he ate, turning red, orange, purple, cheered on by an orchestra of crickets. By the time he carried his plate inside, it had turned a silky black streaked with gold.

He had an arraignment on Monday he was not fully prepared for and a report due in court in the morning. But he knew, as he began to rinse his dishes, that he was going back to the Seaview Jail. He was unreasonably glad that Paula had trusted him enough to give him a picture of Ted, and he was anxious to see if Danny recognized it and where the recognition might lead him.

The truth was, despite Mike's assurances to Paula, the case for Danny's defense was thin. Except for character witnesses he had little to bring to a jury, and he wasn't sure Danny could be a credible witness even if he were to put him on the stand. A jury would only stand for so much prodding by the defense attorney, and Danny was not good at thinking on his own.

The prosecution, on the other hand, had a clear set of Danny Gentry's fingerprints on the murder weapon, not to mention a signed confession—and a grieving husband who said he happened in on the scene while Danny had the knife in his hand.

That was what bothered Mike the most—Ted Raymond's impeccable timing. Mike had read the reports. He knew Raymond could account for his whereabouts for most of the time before the murder.

But if Danny could be trusted to tell the truth, Belinda had been stabbed *before* Danny arrived on the scene. Somebody cunning could have committed the murder and convinced Danny he was to blame.

And then there was the story Paula had told Mike about Belinda's threat to this Wynn Davidson. It seemed unlikely that a bankrupt businessman would take such a threat seriously enough to commit one murder and try for a second—although if Paula Carroll insisted she'd been forced off the road, she very likely had been.

Mike rinsed the last of the dishes and left them in the rack to dry. It was an odd set of circumstances, but he'd certainly heard of murders committed with less motive than that. And his case for Danny Gentry would sure as hell be stronger if he had some other dusty corner to spotlight.

It was a cool, clear night, and Mike was tempted to run the few miles downtown, but it was getting late and it seemed more practical to drive. That way he was sure to get to the jail while Danny was still awake.

The night cop nodded as Mike approached the desk and signed the visitors' log. The last, sweet strains of "*Adeste Fideles*" floated from the rear of the building. It seemed an odd choice more than a month after Christmas, but Mike supposed Danny's repertoire had its limits.

He opted to see his client in his small cell rather than in the visitors' room, and Danny waved happily and lowered the harmonica when the cop let Mike in.

The trifling remains of Danny's dinner were left on a metal tray: a couple of picked-clean chicken bones, a few bits of vegetable, and the last crumbs of a roll. It occurred to Mike that the kid was probably eating better than he did when he was out on the streets. He found the thought disturbing, and he ruffled the youth's dark hair as he moved the tray to the floor and sat on the cot.

"Hi, Mike." Danny sat next to him. "Want me to play somethin' nice for you?"

Mike shook his head. "No, Danny. I came here so we could talk. It's important for you to think very hard and try to remember exactly what happened on the night you found Belinda hurt."

Danny's chin dropped to his chest. "Belinda hurt . . . very bad. . . ."

"Yes, I know. Why did you go there that day, Danny? Why did you go to Belinda's house?"

He glanced up, looking confused, his brows knit together. "I went . . . I went to Belinda's house."

"But why, Danny?" Mike's voice was gentle. "Why did you go to her house?"

Danny thought a minute. The sun broke through. "Danny bring balloons—for Lissa's birthday!"

Mike patted Danny's shoulder. "Okay! Way to go, Danny. That is why you went to Belinda's house. You brought balloons for Lissa's birthday!"

Somewhere, probably in the police report, Mike had read something about a birthday party. . . . Ted Raymond—it was part of his alibi. He said he'd been out looking for a special tablecloth.

"Was there going to be a birthday party for Lissa?" Mike asked. "Did Belinda invite you to a party?"

But the light went out of Danny's eyes. "Balloons. Danny bring balloons."

Mike took a beat, trying hard not to sound exasperated. "Yes, yes. Danny brought balloons. . . ."

And then it occurred to him. The likelihood was

slim that Danny Gentry had thought of balloons on his own. Or had the money to buy them, or knew where to buy them without some kind of direction.

"Danny, this is very important. Did someone tell you to bring balloons for the party?"

Danny nodded.

"Who told you to bring balloons? Was it Belinda? Did Lissa's Mom tell you to bring balloons?"

Danny shook his head. Mike watched him carefully. "Belinda didn't tell you to bring balloons?"

The youth shook his head again.

"Who *did*, Danny? Who told you to bring balloons for the party?"

"The man," Danny shrugged his shoulders, as if anybody smart should know that. "The man give Danny money. He say, 'You be there five o'clock. Not one minute late.'"

The man. Mike felt his heartbeat quicken. The man had told Danny to bring balloons—told him to be at Belinda's house at *exactly* five o'clock. Why? Because the murder would be committed within minutes before that? Because Danny was so easy to manipulate?

Danny was looking at him with absolute trust. Mike looked straight into his eyes. "Who was the man, Danny? Who was it? What was the man's name? Do you know it?"

Danny shook his head.

"You don't know his name."

The youth shook his head again.

"Was it someone you know?"

Danny nodded.

Mike waited, but Danny remained silent. Finally he reached into his jacket pocket and took out the picture of Ted Raymond. He held it up directly in front of Danny. "Take your time, Danny. Then tell me. Is this the man?"

Danny stared at the photograph wide-eyed. And then he began to shriek.

The television droned on, but Paula, lying on the living room sofa, could not have said what was on the air. Lissa, who'd fallen asleep an hour ago, was nestled in the crook of her good arm, and Paula stared, mesmerized as always, at the innocent curve of her little cheek and the shadow of her long lashes. Belinda had called her "the littlest miracle. . . ."

"She really is, you know. In a million years, I wouldn't have believed it. She really is a little miracle."

Paula had laughed. *"I don't know about that, but she sure has a healthy appetite."*

They'd been sitting on the patio of Belinda and Ted's apartment just outside San Diego. Belinda had the baby wrapped in a blanket to shield her against the February cold, and Paula held her close and watched her suck furiously on the nipple of the pink and white bottle.

"Ted is crazy about her," Belinda'd said.

"Yes, I know. And I'm glad."

"It will be such fun to watch her grow up."

"I hope she has a best friend like you."

Belinda had paused. *"What should she call you?"*

"Not 'Aunt Paula.' That sounds dopey."

"Well, what then?"

". . . I don't know." Paula'd thought a minute. *"What's wrong with just my name?"*

And so it had been decided, as it was to this day, that Lissa was simply to call her Paula. And the three of them—Paula, Belinda, and Ted—would have been hard put to make a decision as to which of them loved that baby best.

Now, holding her, Paula came face to face with feelings that were difficult to deal with. She was twenty-seven years old and the notion of herself as somebody's mommy held more appeal than it ever had. . . .

It wasn't until Lissa stirred that she realized the phone was ringing. Gently extricating her arm, she glanced at her watch. Ten-thirty. Turning slightly, she reached behind her and felt for the telephone on the table.

She would have been willing to bet it was Ted, to tell her when he would be home. But the rasping voice had a chilling familiarity: "Some . . . people . . . just . . . won't . . . learn."

CHAPTER

22

Strangely, Paula was less frightened by the late-night phone call than she was galvanized into action.

Ted had come home shortly after the call. He'd seemed considerably calmer and she didn't even want to speculate as to whether or not he'd been the caller. If she had, she would have found it nearly impossible to go away and leave Lissa in his care. As it was, the one thing she knew for sure was that she had to get back to San Francisco.

Early on Friday, while Lissa was in preschool, she telephoned her agent. "Zach, hello, it's me, Paula. . . . Well, I've felt better, but I want to go home. . . . Yes. . . . I'm happy you're happy. . . ."

She asked Zach to call a local domestic agency and get someone to stay with her for a while. She still needed help getting dressed and getting around, and she would need someone who could drive.

"Call Nally at the station, too," she told Zach. "Tell him I'm coming home. The bruises on my face are fading fast, and if he thinks he can put up with the cast on my arm, I'll be back on the air Monday night."

She called her own doctor and made an appointment for early Monday morning. If there was anything he could do to get her out of at least one of her casts, her life would be a lot simpler.

She was about to dial a limousine company and hire a car to drive her home on Saturday when the doorbell rang. She pushed herself up out of the chair, proud of herself because it seemed to be getting easier, and made her way to the front door.

For safety's sake—was she getting skittish?—she peered through the sheer curtain on the narrow window in the hall. She saw a florist's delivery truck parked in the driveway, and a fresh-faced kid holding a huge basket of flowers and pressing the doorbell with his elbow.

Smiling, she unlocked the door and opened it. It was the biggest floral bouquet she'd ever seen.

"For Paula Carroll," the kid said, looking at her uncertainly.

"That's me," she said. "That's absolutely beautiful. Do me a favor and bring it inside."

She had him place the flowers in the center of the dining room table, and she scrawled her signature on the delivery sheet he held for her.

When he'd gone, she stood staring at the mass of flowers, yellow chrysanthemums, red roses, and white cymbidiums, then she poked around among the greenery and baby's breath until she found a card.

It was awkward opening the envelope with one hand and her teeth, but at last she could read the card:

Duty calls, or I'd be by your side. "I Only
Have Eyes for You."

                          Love, Sam

She smiled. He really did like the old love songs.
She reached him at his office. "They're just beautiful."

"Not nearly as beautiful as you."

"You're going to spoil me."

"Lord, I hope so. Can we start with dinner tonight?"

Paula thought about it. "That's very tempting. But
I feel like I'm cast in stone. And anyway, I want to
get an early start tomorrow. I'm going to hire a car
and go home."

Sam was adamant. "Hire a car, my foot. Tell me
what time you want me there. I'll bring the Lincoln.
It's plenty roomy, and you can leave the driving to
me."

Highway Patrolman Hank Chandler brought a
cup of coffee to his desk in a cubbyhole at the CHP
office in Seaview. It was probably useless, but he'd
gotten in the habit of checking each day's teletypes
for hit-and-run incidents bearing any similarity to
the one Paula Carroll had described.

For the hundredth time, he wished she'd been able
to get a license number for the car that hit her. It
would have made things simple, and he would have
been all too happy to be the one to bring her solid
information. As it was, his job was not only tedious,
it was like looking for a flea on a hound.

His teletype and broadcast on the night of the
accident had yielded nothing at all—not surprising,
given the skimpy description Paula had been able to

provide—and the more time that went by, the less the likelihood that the suspect vehicle would be found abandoned.

They had a few paint scrapings from Paula's car, but they would be useless unless or until they had a suspect vehicle to match them against. About the only good news, as far as Chandler was concerned, was that fragments of headlight glass taken from the scene were determined to be Ford product, so Paula's observation that it might have been a Bonneville could just be on the mark.

Chandler tilted back in his chair and sipped the lukewarm coffee. The chances of finding the suspect vehicle were probably slim to none. But, hey, a lady like Paula Carroll was worth a little extra trouble. Smoothing his hair back, he put down his coffee mug and hunched forward over his desk to look at last night's teletypes.

Mike took the two flights of stairs to the police station three steps at a time and shaded his eyes as he walked into the dim room from the glare outside.

He was still reeling from Danny's reaction the night before to the photo he'd shown him of Ted Raymond. The kid had freaked out, no doubt about that, and no amount of reasoning or reassurance had been able to calm him down.

Not that it meant Raymond was the killer, or even that he was the man who'd arranged for Danny to arrive at the murder scene at five o'clock. Not that Raymond necessarily even knew it was going to be a murder scene at the time the arrangements were made. It was tempting to jump to that kind of conclusion, but the simple fact might be that Danny was reacting to the picture of a man who had beat him nearly senseless in that kitchen. Mike could only hope that Danny would soon calm down enough to make himself understood.

Inside the station, Felipe Garza was sitting on a scarred wooden desktop. It appeared he was telling some hilarious story to a couple of very attentive dispatchers. His white teeth flashed, his blue shirt was crisp, and his tie was knotted just so.

Felipe, too, had been a member of the Seaview High class of '84. He was a jerk then, he was a jerk now. Some things never changed. Mike rounded a corner to the detective's unit and peered into Natt-linger's office.

It was empty save for the furniture, the dusty plastic plant and a collection of candy wrappers on the floor. Mike debated leaving a note, which likely would never be found among the debris, but he turned, startled but unaccountably pleased, at the sound of the husky voice.

"Hey, counselor, looking for me?"

Mike looked into the beefy face. "Yeah. How are ya?"

"Disagreeable, as usual. What's on your mind besides developmentally disabled clients and errant husbands?"

Mike grinned and perched on the desktop as the big man lowered himself into his chair. He waited until the wheezes and squeaks subsided. "Neither. You lose. Now you owe me one."

Nattlinger grunted. "Oh, yeah?"

"Yeah."

"What's it worth to you?"

"How about lunch?"

The big man shrugged. "That much, eh? Okay, counselor, whaddya need?"

"I need you to run a make on a guy named Wynn Davidson. That's W-y-n-n. He owns a company called Duncan Associates in Las Vegas, but let's see if there's anything on him in California."

He flashed Nattlinger an ingratiating smile. "Oh, and if you should happen to know someone in Nevada . . ."

Nattlinger responded with a moronic grin. "Yeah, yeah. I dig."

Lissa's blue eyes glistened with tears, and her lower lip trembled. "But I don't want you to go home, Paula. I want you to stay here!"

Paula sighed. "I know you do, sweetheart. I wish I could stay, too. You're the best little nurse anybody could have. But I have to get back to work."

Lissa flounced down on the guest room bed, her little arms crossed in front of her.

Paula lowered herself into the peach-colored chair. "I'll only be away for seven days. You can cross the days off on a calendar, and I'll be back next Saturday."

A long pause. "Dr. Irvin says I can talk about my mommy anytime I want."

"Well, of course, you can."

"But my mommy went away. She isn't ever coming back. Why can't you be my new mommy?"

It was Paula's turn to hesitate. "Because you can't get new mommies the way you get new socks. Even if I could stay here and take care of you all the time, you would still remember your mommy. And you should."

Lissa swung her legs. "But who will take care of me?"

"Your daddy. And Mrs. Morrissey. You'll go home

with her and Tiffany sometimes, and your daddy will bring you home before dinnertime."

A hint of mischief glinted in Lissa's eyes. "You can't go home if you don't pack your things. And you can't do it all by yourself. So there! What if I won't help!"

Paula smiled. "Pretty please? Please with sugar on top?"

"Pancake syrup!"

"All right, pancake syrup. Now will you help me pack?"

A shy smile. "Oh, okay. How many days till you come back?"

"Seven." Paula rooted around in her purse until she came up with a Hallmark date book. With her good left hand, she opened it flat and held it for Lissa to see. "These are the days I'm going to be gone. You can mark each one with a crayon. And when you get to this one—see, it says Sat-ur-day— I'll be on my way back for the weekend."

Mollified, Lissa got Paula's small suitcase and opened it on the bed. They were nearly through packing when the downstairs door opened and Ted called out that he was home.

Scrambling off the bed, smiling happily, Lissa ran downstairs. "Daddy, Daddy! I got a smiley face on my alphabet paper! And guess what? Paula's going home!"

CHAPTER

23

There was something reassuring about the familiar landscape rolling by outside. Paula stared out the car window, feeling herself relax.

"Are you comfortable?" Sam asked her. "I can adjust the air-conditioning."

"No, I'm fine. It's perfect," she assured him, tilting her head back against the leather seat to make the most of the panoramic view.

Lissa had watched stoically, her hands at her sides, when Sam helped Paula into his car. But she'd reached up and given her a hug and a kiss and promised to be waiting for her next Saturday.

Ted, for his part, had been something of an enigma, hoisting Paula's bag into the car, pecking her on the cheek and wishing her luck, but tonelessly, as though he wished she were already someplace else.

Paula wished she could rid herself of the feeling that Ted was watching her all the time, as though if he could only read her mind, he would know what he had to do next.

He was not a strong person. Belinda had known that, too. But he blossomed under the right direction. A vision of him holding the infant Lissa brought a smile to Paula's lips.

They had packed the baby into her stroller and traipsed through the zoo in Balboa Park. Paula and Belinda had gone into the gift shop, and when they came out, Ted was standing by the stroller, holding a screaming Lissa in his arms. The expression on his face suggested rising panic, and Paula's instinct had been to reach for the baby.

But Belinda had put a hand on her arm and strolled over to her husband. *"Put her over your shoulder, honey. Pat her back. She probably needs to burp."*

Ted had looked down at the bundle in his arms. *"H-how do I do that?"*

"Easy. Support her head with one hand while you lift her up with the other."

Ted had looked from one to the other of the women, as though the task he'd been given was impossible. But in the next minute, he'd slung Lissa over his shoulder. She quieted, and he'd grinned in triumph.

"Something funny?" Sam must have been watching Paula as he drove.

"No, not really." In fact, the memory had triggered a sobering thought. "Sam"—she leaned in closer toward him, so he could hear her more easily over the wind—"you're a friend of Ted's. You've stuck with him through . . . all this. What do you make of his behavior? I mean—does he seem . . . normal to you, or is he acting a little erratic?"

Sam seemed to consider the question. "Actually, I've been worried about Ted, too. He always seems to be . . . looking back over his shoulder, as though he were expecting—I don't know what."

Paula thought about it. Yes, there was that. Well, guilt would certainly cause a person to look back over his shoulder. She pressed her lips together. Guilt over what he had done to his wife—or guilt over his part in the refinery mess?

"Of course, to be fair," Sam was saying, "he's under a tremendous amount of stress. His wife is gone, he found her butchered body in their kitchen, he has full responsibility for Lissa—and he'll undoubtedly have to testify at the trial of the murderer. That won't be easy, having to relive the whole thing all over again. . . ."

They were coming into San Francisco. The Golden Gate Bridge loomed in front of them, and Paula, as always, marveled at the splendor of the City by the Bay.

Sam slowed to pay the toll.

"You think Danny Gentry is guilty," Paula murmured.

"Yes, Paula, I do. I've given a lot of thought to what you told me about Ted—his possible involvement with Duncan Associates and all—but somehow, it—I don't know. It doesn't wash. I don't think Ted's capable of murder. And certainly not because Belinda was angry at him over his dragging his feet on the site inspection."

She tilted her face up to stare into the clouds. Hearing it like that made it sound so . . . trivial. But even if Mike Shaffer were wrong, even if Danny killed Belinda—who had broken into Paula's mailbox? Who had forced her off the road and nearly killed her?

"And by the way," Sam told her as they hurtled over the bridge, "I've done some checking on your Wynn Davidson. Have you ever called him?"

Paula shook her head. "There didn't seem to be much point. What was I going to ask him? Did you have anything to do with the death of my friend Belinda? With having me forced off the shoulder of a highway?"

Sam chuckled. "You have a point there. But I did have some bright people take a look at him. From all reports, he's a clever business type not above a little chicanery. But there's no indication he's ever been involved in anything more serious than crime-by-paper."

Before she could respond, he looked over at her. "Paula, my dear, I need directions from here. I don't have the slightest idea where you live."

They ended up stopping for lunch at a French café in Ghirardelli Square, then Paula directed him down Polk Street and across Green to her apartment on the lower level of a converted Victorian row house near Russian Hill.

She felt a surge of affection—and a feeling of relief—as they pulled into her driveway. Humble or not, she was glad to be home among her own familiar things.

She handed Sam the key and then preceded him through the foyer to an airy, high-ceilinged living room comfortably furnished in Country French in shades of mauve and gray.

"It's lovely," he told her. "Warm and elegant, just like its owner."

"Why, thank you, sir," she indicated a chair by the

fireplace. "Make yourself at home. I'd like to take a quick, reassuring little tour and get the messages off my machine."

To her great relief, everything in the apartment appeared to be just as she'd left it. There were two messages on her answering machine: Her car, which had been towed to a Seaview garage, was ready to be picked up. And an Amy Takehara from the Welch Domestic Agency would stop by to be interviewed at three o'clock.

The city, as always, was cooler than the suburbs. Sam started a roaring fire and made coffee, which they sipped as they talked. He told her about his boyhood north of Seattle, where his father had started his lumber business, and about what he called his *philosophical* years at Berkeley, when he'd nearly decided to chuck the family business for more pastoral pursuits somewhere in the backwoods of Oregon.

"Sometimes," he told her, "I think I might have been happier in a beard and a log cabin. . . . But old Dad convinced me that a penny earned was better than a penny owed."

Paula smiled, warmed by the sadness in his handsomely chiseled face and was truly surprised, when the doorbell rang, at how quickly the time had gone by.

Cast in stone or not, Sam told her, as he went to answer the door, she would need dinner, and he planned to come back and pick her up at seven sharp.

Amy Takehara was twenty-four years old and had worked primarily as a nanny, mostly for the children of foreign diplomats living in San Francisco. But she happened to be between assignments, she explained, and this temporary position as a personal assistant seemed to be tailor-made.

She was pretty, trim, and dark-haired with friendly, open features. She exuded an air of warmth and efficiency, and Paula liked her right off. By the time they'd gotten Paula bathed and dressed, they were chatting away like old friends.

Mike spent part of the morning in the law library, researching corporate structure. He had the nagging feeling he was missing something, but he couldn't put his finger on what it was.

At noon he met Celia at the pancake house for lunch. They had Russian blini with sour cream.

"Not as good as Lou's." Celia shrugged. "But then, I don't have to wash the dishes."

She had met with Danny several times, she told Mike. There was no question of his diminished capacity. But he understood the nature of the crime he was charged with, and he understood the role of his attorney. There was no reason, as far as she could determine, why he should not be allowed to stand trial.

"The question in my mind is whether to put him on the stand." Mike spread sour cream over his blini. "I'm convinced he didn't kill Belinda. She was his friend. There was nothing sexual in it. But he gets hysterical when he remembers the crime scene, when he talks about Belinda and all the blood. I think he just feels guilty because he couldn't help her—but I'm not sure a jury would be convinced."

Celia nodded. "It *is* a dilemma. I plan to point out a history of nonviolence, and the evidence is mostly circumstantial. But if a good prosecutor has at him on the stand, he may reduce him to a blubbering mass of jelly."

"And yet if I don't let him testify, there's a good chance they'll convict him on the evidence alone. Especially if Ted Raymond, the lone witness, plays the grieving husband to the hilt."

Celia looked at him. "My dear friend, do I detect a note of sarcasm regarding the widower?"

Mike paused while the waitress poured coffee. "I didn't want to influence you in any way, Celia, before you'd drawn your own conclusions about Danny. But the kid's defense will be a lot stronger if I can go after Raymond on the stand."

He told her about the mixed signals he was picking up from Paula Carroll. About Danny's freaking out when he looked at the photo Mike had shown him of Ted Raymond.

Celia shrugged. "The man beat him pretty badly. I should think that could be cause for hysterics."

"I know." Mike drummed his fingers on the table-top. "But there's more. I just haven't found it yet. . . ."

He listened to the tremor in the man's voice. "I told you not to call me here."

"I know. I—I know. But I've been thinking. There are some things I—don't understand."

"You know everything you need to know," he said coldly. "You have a rock-solid alibi."

"But Paula—"

"You needn't worry about Paula."

"And that lawyer. If he knows about Duncan. . . ."

He shook his head. He should have known. Some-thing was going to have to be done.

CHAPTER

24

"I feel like I've been let out of prison," Paula said, walking out into the chilly sunshine on Monday morning.

Amy Takehara grinned. "You must be ten pounds lighter!"

Paula's doctor, consulting her X rays, had been pleased with his patient's progress.

"You're young and healthy," he'd told her. "The bones are knitting well. Let's see what we can do."

In the end, he agreed the arm cast could be shed—if Paula would agree to keep the arm in a sling and keep it relatively immobile. As for the cast on her leg, it could be shortened and streamlined and a walking heel could be added so she could, within reason, put her weight on the leg and get around a lot more easily.

Amy had helped her into a blue silk suit that made her feel slim and sexy, and they'd brushed her tawny hair back into a sleek chignon held with a gold clip. It was the first time in a week—except for Saturday night—that Paula had worn anything but jeans or bathrobes, and she toyed with the notion of stopping by Sam's office to show off her new persona.

Saturday evening he had taken her to the exquisite revolving dining room at the top of the St. Francis Hotel, where they'd dined on lobster and sipped champagne as they gazed out over the city. She'd made herself as presentable as possible in a long sleeved gown of flowing green chiffon, and if the presence of her two ugly casts bothered Sam, he'd done a masterful job of hiding it.

Sunday she had spent quietly, reading the papers and catching up on long overdue correspondence. But this morning she felt wonderful, and she was gratified to find she needed considerably less help getting into the rented car. As Amy pulled out into the light, mid-morning traffic, Paula rummaged in her purse for the San Francisco business card Sam had given her the other evening. When they passed Geary on the way to the studio, she made a sudden decision.

"Turn right at the next corner," she told Amy. "I want to make a brief stop."

They passed a succession of fashionable, low-rise business buildings, primarily housing legal and accounting firms. When they reached the number Paula was looking for, Amy pulled smoothly to the curb. Paula put a restraining hand on Amy's arm and managed to let herself out of the car.

She looked back triumphantly. "Ta-daa! Was that brilliant?" She grinned. "I won't be a minute."

Discreet gold lettering on the heavy oak door read, *Mac and Lady Mac, Superior Sportswear*. Paula raised an eyebrow. Sam had told her he'd diversified his holdings, but sportswear! She'd had no idea!

She would have asked about it if he hadn't been standing right up front at the antique French reception desk, ankle deep in plush burgundy carpeting and beaming at the sight of her as she entered.

"Paula!" He moved toward her and took her in at a glance, pleasure mirrored in his warm, gray eyes. "You Are Love," he whispered to her in low tones, and Paula laughed, imagining him, in costume on some magnificent stage, breaking into light-operatic song.

"I'm on my way to the studio," she told him. "And I'm sure you have a million things to do. But I just came from the doctor's office, and I thought I'd stop by for just a minute and show off my streamlined self."

The receptionist, a well-tailored woman in her thirties, was looking at them with naked curiosity, but if Sam noticed, he chose to ignore it. He looked deeply into Paula's eyes, so deeply and so long that she felt an embarrassing stirring.

"I have to leave," she faltered finally.

"We could take an early lunch."

She shook her head. "No. I really do have to get to the studio."

"Well then"—he followed her to the door—"can I pick you up at the studio? At seven?"

She nodded, feeling beautiful and valued. "Yes. I'll see you then."

It appeared February was settling in with a vengeance. The butter-colored streets had turned gray, and the heavy mist that had hung around all morning was turning into an honest rain.

Mike Shaffer watched it through the window from his desk in the public defender's office. He didn't mind. The arroyo—in fact, the whole canyon beyond his deck—was overdue for a good soaking.

But he felt vaguely out of sorts, and he wasn't sure why—except that he was due back in court with Danny soon, and he wasn't nearly ready to proceed.

He picked up a pencil and twirled it aimlessly. Danny had calmed down somewhat. But he couldn't—or wouldn't—explain why he'd gotten hysterical at the sight of Ted Raymond's photograph, and neither would he positively identify him as the man who had ordered him to pick up balloons and be at the Raymond house at five o'clock on the day of Belinda's death.

Mike had read the police reports again and again. He knew Ted had been in Sam Pierce's office in the hours just preceding Belinda's murder; that he'd stopped somewhere, allegedly to pick up a table-cloth, and then gone directly home. But he could have instructed Danny at any time—even several days before the murder—to deliver those balloons precisely at five.

How angry had Belinda been when she learned her husband had stalled on the refinery inspection? Angry enough to goad him into believing murder was the only way to win her silence?

It didn't seem likely. Unless, of course, Paula Carroll had seen only the tip of the iceberg. Unless Belinda knew about—or suspected—a deeper connection between her husband and Wynn Davidson. A payoff, perhaps? Could Ted have accepted money from Duncan Associates to drag his feet on that site inspection?

Mike felt his senses quicken. Now several things made more sense. Including the alleged attempt on

Paula's life, especially if Davidson had reason to believe she knew everything Belinda had known.

He tapped the pencil hard on the desktop. Could he get Paula on the stand? Could he get her to testify, at Danny Gentry's trial, that the dead woman's husband—with or without the blessings of an accomplice—had a motive for murder?

Not likely, he told himself all the while he dialed the Raymonds' number. Paula had likely given Mike the photograph because she knew she wouldn't stand in his way if he had anything solid against Ted. But he had nothing solid, time was running short, and he wasn't sure where to look next.

The little girl answered the telephone. "Hello, who is this?"

"Hello, Lissa. This is Mike Shaffer. Do you remember who I am?"

"Sure, I do," the little voice piped. "You carried me up on your shoulders!"

Mike smiled. "So I did. Lissa, can Paula come to the telephone?"

Lissa giggled. "Paula's not here! Sam took her home to Safracisco!"

"Oh."

"But my daddy's here. Do you want to talk to him?"

"No. No, that's all right. I'll talk to Paula another time. You take care."

"I will. Bye!"

The security guard must have called upstairs the moment Paula and Amy stepped into the elevator, because when they emerged, the whole KSFO crew was standing in the corridor and applauding.

"Looking good, Paula!"

"Way to go, babe!"

"Missed ya! Welcome back!"

And Rollie, standing head and shoulders above the others. "Don't you worry your pretty little head, honey. Rollie's magic fingers will do wonders!"

A surge of gratitude swelled in her throat. She blinked back tears. "Thanks. What a bunch! I love you all, too. Oh! And this is Amy Takehara. She's helping me out until I can get around by myself. Be nice to her. She doesn't know you like I do!"

The crowd dispersed amid cheers and jeers.

"Hello, Amy!"

"Welcome aboard!"

"Hey, she's gorgeous! Give her a script!"

Her producer stepped forward. "Welcome back, Paula. It hasn't been the same without you."

Paula thought guiltily of Stu Snyder. Would that offer be coming from network? And if it did—she didn't want to think about it. "Thanks, Nally. It's good to be back. I'll be in my dressing room. If you see Deirdre, would you send her around to see me?"

She showed Amy around the crowded corridors, the soundstages, the makeup rooms, the kitchen. "Pay attention. There'll be a test later. People are always getting lost around here."

When she got to her dressing room, Amy helped her out of her suit and into a pink nylon makeup robe.

Betty Lou knocked and handed her a script. "Slow news day."

"Happy to hear it."

Amy was on her way out for sandwiches and coffee when Deirdre appeared in the doorway.

A big smile deepened the woman's dimples. She

hugged Paula warmly. "Hi, we missed you. Are you okay?"

Paula nodded. "As okay as I can be under the circumstances."

Deirdre flashed her an understanding smile. "So. Do you want to talk about it?"

"I don't think so. Not yet." Paula moved clothing off the small sofa and indicated a place for Deirdre to sit. "I just wondered if you'd gotten anywhere on the Seaview refinery mess."

Deirdre shook her head. "Not really. This Wynn Davidson is one slippery eel. Duncan Associates is out of business and out of their suite of offices in Las Vegas. And I can't make contact with a single one of the corporation's other officers."

Paula thought a minute. "A Nevada corporation doing business in California has to be listed with our Secretary of State's office, doesn't it?"

"Check." Deirdre nodded. "But whoever those people are, they sure don't want to be found."

It occurred to Paula that Duncan Associates might be a link in a larger chain, a small-fish subsidiary of some parent corporation that was a faster and more adroit swimmer.

Surprised at the agility with which she was able to get up from her seat, she reached for her purse and rummaged around for the number Sam Pierce had found for her.

"Well"—she handed the slip of paper to Deirdre—"a good friend tells me this is Wynn Davidson's personal number. I'm not quite sure just where it will get you. But here. If you want it, it's yours."

CHAPTER
~25~

"Who was that?"

Ted hadn't realized it but he must have shouted, because Lissa nearly jumped out of her skin.

"M-Mike," she whispered.

He tried to quiet the thunderstorm in his gut. "Mike. Mike who?"

Lissa shrugged, her lower lip quivering. "I don't 'member his other name. Just Mike. He carried me on his shoulders."

"Is it Mike Shaffer?"

Lissa nodded slowly.

He gritted his teeth. *The bastard! The one who was defending the half-wit! Carrying Lissa on his shoulders!* "Did he ask for Paula?"

She nodded again.

He bent down and took her by the arm. "This Mike"—he worked to keep his voice even—"have you seen him here—at our house?"

"Yes."

But Lissa wasn't here the other day when he'd

caught Shaffer here with Paula. "How many times was he here in this house?"

A shrug. "I don't know."

"Was it here that he carried you up on his shoulders?"

"No. Paula took me to the ice cream store. Then we took a walk and my feet got tired, and that's when he picked me up."

Another gale force whipped through Ted's stomach. *So Paula's been seeing him all along!*

"Daddy, you're hurting me!" Tears welled in Lissa's frightened eyes.

He released her immediately, saw the color return to the white spot where he'd pinched the skin of her arm. Then he crushed her to him. "Oh, honey, Daddy's sorry. You know I never meant to hurt you."

She remained in his arms for a long moment, but he could feel the tension in her little body. Finally he released her. "Daddy's so sorry, Lissa. I've been— well, I haven't been feeling too well. Maybe a good game would make us both feel better. How about Chinese Checkers? Or Chutes and Ladders?"

Lissa shook her head. "I have to finish my number paper for school tomorrow." She turned away and headed for the stairs. "I'm going up to my room."

Ted watched her trudge up the stairs, her little back stiff. Poor little Lissa. He hadn't meant to hurt her. He would never want to do that. . . . He hoped Paula hadn't been poisoning her against him. . . . *Paula!* He clenched his fists.

She could never leave well alone, never! Like the time back at college when that big basketball player keeled over and everybody thought it was his heart. But Paula the news junkie had dug deep, had managed to turn up a cocaine habit—a habit that damned near devastated the kid's family and almost got the league championships canceled. . . .

And now she can't leave this alone, either. She thinks she's got the whole thing figured out. And she's cozying up to that public defender, shoring up a case against me. . . .

Ted began to sweat. He could try talking to her, try to make her understand. God, he missed Belinda, too. *He was so sorry! Didn't Paula know that?*

Paula leaned back, closed her eyes, and gave herself up to Rollie's ministrations. If anyone could camouflage the last of her bruises and make her look beautiful, he could.

It had started to rain. Paula could hear it thrumming against the outside of the building. She found the sound relaxing. Her skin felt cool as Rollie patted astringent on her face.

"Paula, phone for you!" It was Betty Lou's voice.

"I don't want it. If it's Zach, I'll call him later."

"It isn't. It's some other guy. He says it's urgent. But then, with guys it usually is."

Paula considered. Sam? Not likely. She'd already agreed to see him tonight. Ted? Lissa! Her heart leaped. "Okay, transfer the call in here."

It was Mike Shaffer. Paula wavered between annoyance and relief.

"I hope you don't mind my calling you at work," he told her. "I didn't know where else to reach you."

"I'm busy—"

"I understand. But I need to see you. It could—this is very important. I'll be happy to drive into San Francisco. Just tell me when and where."

Paula hesitated. She hadn't exactly played fair with the public defender. The one thing she was relatively sure of was that Danny had not killed Belinda. Yet she'd told Mike Shaffer just enough to get him to point his cannons elsewhere, and now that he might be aiming in the right direction she was holding on to all the ammunition.

"All right," she said at last. "Tomorrow afternoon. I have some dead time between about two and four in the afternoon. Do you know where the studio is?"

"No, but I'll find it."

"Okay. I'll see you then."

"Sounds intriguing, *ma chère*," Rollie tilted her face up and began to apply foundation. "A new man in your life?"

"Could be," she said coyly. *But not the man on the telephone.*

She smiled at the thought of Mike as a love interest. Heavens, she'd known him since high school. He hadn't been sophisticated enough for her then, and he was not sophisticated now.

She shifted in her chair. She had to admit, there was a certain appeal in his grown-up, rugged good looks. But he was beer and pretzels on a warm afternoon, when all she'd ever wanted was champagne and caviar on a soft, moonlit night.

Like Sam, she thought, warming at the thought that she would see him in a couple of hours— saddened by the fact that she would have to leave him early in order to come back and do the ten o'clock broadcast.

Oh well, she told herself ruefully, it was a little tough to be romantic with a sling and a cast in her way.

But Sam would wait. The right time would come. She felt the color rise in her cheeks.

• • •

But by the time Sam picked her up at seven o'clock, she was sorry she'd made the date.

She'd forgotten how irritating the hot lights could be when you'd sat in them for over an hour. She'd flubbed up in rehearsal and flubbed up even worse on the air during the six o'clock broadcast. And she definitely regretted making the appointment to see Mike Shaffer tomorrow.

". . . You're a million miles away." Sam's voice was gentle.

She looked up, startled. "Sorry."

"Maybe this wasn't a good idea. Shall I take you back to the studio?"

Paula smoothed the white tablecloth in their booth at a Hungarian café near the studio. "No, I'll be fine. It's just—I don't know. Lots of things settling in at once."

He smiled, putting a hand over hers. "Look, I've been thinking about what you told me. And I guess—I don't know—I guess I just don't want to believe that Ted could possibly have had anything to do with Belinda's death."

She sighed. "I know. . . ."

"He loved Belinda. He's a good man. And he's the only parent Lissa has left."

The words were a knife in Paula's heart. "Sam—"

He squeezed her hand. "Paula, there's more. . . . I'm concerned for your personal safety. Somebody took a run at you once. Suppose they try it again. . . ."

"But—"

"Please. Let me finish." He looked desperate. "You must know how much . . . I care for you. I couldn't stand it—I simply couldn't—if anything were to happen to you."

She felt torn in two. "I appreciate that, Sam. But I can't turn away from the truth—"

"Yes, you can. Let me do it for you. Money can open a lot of doors."

She stared at him.

"Paula, I'll make you a bargain. Do nothing that might put you in jeopardy. In return, I'll have this Davidson investigated clear back to the time he was in diapers. I'll find out about Duncan. And how Ted was involved. I'll search the truth out for you."

She smiled, touched. "You would do that for me."

He nodded. "And more. You must know how much I care for you."

A waiter approached. "Would you like to start with some wine?"

Paula looked at her menu. The place smelled wonderful. All at once she realized she was starving.

CHAPTER

26

Rain thudded against his windshield in thick, heavy sheets. Mike debated pulling off the road. His wipers weren't cutting it, and it was foolish to take chances even if it meant he'd be late getting to San Francisco.

Squinting into his rearview mirror, he edged toward the right lane, but as suddenly as it had come the torrent subsided, and he could see a little more of the road ahead of him.

Mike thought it over. It still might make sense to wait the storm out off the highway. He could call Paula, explain what happened, and let her know he'd be late. But she'd only given him a two-hour window, and he'd had to cajole her into that.

He had spent the better part of yesterday afternoon visiting with Danny Gentry; talking to him, trying to soothe his fears, even getting him to play his harmonica. Finally Danny had been able to describe how Ted had beaten him in the kitchen—

how he'd bashed Danny's head against the kitchen counter again and again and again.

But he hadn't been able to tell Mike with any certainty that it was Ted who'd asked him to bring the balloons. "The man . . . ," he'd repeated again and again in a slow, maddening singsong until Mike had finally reached the end of his patience and called the interview quits.

Mike had the feeling Paula knew—or suspected— more than she had told him. And her testimony on the stand, if he could get her to commit to it, could tip the balance in Danny's favor if he had to stand trial.

Mike drummed his fingertips against the steering wheel. There was little traffic on the highway. What the heck? He'd come this far. He might as well try to tough it out.

Hank Chandler shook the water off his helmet and hung it on a peg near his desk. His yellow slicker was already pooling water on the asphalt tile at his feet.

It was the kind of day every highway patrolman hated: one accident after another. What with the hard rain and poor visibility out there, he thought, it was a wonder there's been enough of a respite at all for Chandler to make it back to the office.

Running a hand through his thick crew cut, he decided to go get some coffee. With luck, he might finagle a half hour or so to go over the most recent hit-and-runs.

He was standing by the dispatcher's station pouring coffee when the call came in. Without waiting for orders, he put down the coffeepot and ran for his helmet and slicker.

• • •

Deirdre was standing on a rocky, windswept bluff overlooking the Dinsmore Reservoir. She was wearing a tan trenchcoat and a corduroy rain hat and one of her hands was wrapped firmly around a microphone while the other hand was making a valiant effort to hold onto an oversized umbrella.

Thirty feet below her, if she squinted through the downpour, she could make out a blur of activity: yellow-slickered rescue workers, a couple of black rubber boats, and the swirling, angry, white-capped water.

"Right below where I'm standing," she shouted, "in this rain-swollen arm of the Dinsmore Reservoir—hey, hold it, Izzy, stop rolling tape. There is no way I'm hanging onto this umbrella. You can come up and get it, or I'm letting it go. It's either the umbrella or the story!"

Izzy peered up over the top of the minicam and made a jerking motion with his head. Deirdre took it to mean "ditch the umbrella." Looking around her, she noticed a small crevice two feet to her left side. She clambered over to reach it, jammed the umbrella handle between two boulders, then braced herself, shoved her free hand gratefully into a pocket and started her spiel again.

"Below me, in this rain-swollen arm of the Dinsmore Reservoir, efforts continue to find a twelve-year-old boy who, friends say, was swept into the channel when he went chasing after his runaway bicycle as they were returning home from school. . . ."

Trying, without the protection of the umbrella, to look as if she weren't getting soaked, Deirdre battled the wind to deliver a few more sentences into her microphone about who the boy was, how many agencies had rescue workers on site and what they thought their chances were of finding the boy and fishing him out safely.

It was to be promo footage for the six o'clock broadcast, three hours away. If the boy had been rescued by then, the segment would conclude with a recap of his condition, interviews with rescue workers and interviews with the boy's parents if they were available. If he had not been found, and rescue attempts were continuing, then the footage Izzy had just videotaped would be aired as recent on-site coverage with updates as they were feasible.

By the time Izzy gave her the cut sign, Deirdre was soaked through. She was cold and tired, but exhilarated, as always, at being part of news as it happened. From vantage points on similar bluffs overlooking the reservoir, reporters from other stations were battling the elements to bring the story to their viewers.

From where she stood, she could see that some of the more dauntless news teams had insinuated themselves down to the water's edge. One reporter seemed to be thrusting a microphone into the face of a resisting rescue worker.

It was tempting, Deirdre knew from her own experience, to go after the most dangerous angle—to be the one who scoops the competition and gets the prime footage that every station is going to end up using. But KSFO had its own *"responsible news coverage policy,"* and Deirdre knew better than to violate its danger parameters if she wanted to keep her job.

But she was still honing her news instincts, and

she never failed to be totally fascinated by the way other reporters did things.

Below her she could see Izzy fitting a protective cover over the minicam, his shaggy gray mane whipping in the breeze as he bent over his gear. Shivering, she leaned over to retrieve the umbrella, which was still wedged between the rocks.

She never saw the stocky figure creeping up behind her. She felt nothing at all until her head exploded as it smashed into a boulder. She felt nothing at all as she tumbled, weightless, down the steep and rocky embankment.

CHAPTER

27

Paula reached an irritating conclusion while Amy was helping her dress. She had a closet full of suits and dresses perfectly tailored for the camera. But for as long as her arm must remain in a sling, it would be on camera, too, and she owned an appallingly small stock of scarves with which to dress it for the occasion.

"I think"—she held still as Amy zipped her into a coral-colored wool sheath—"we had better stop at Capwell's on the way to the studio and pick up a coral print scarf—and a handful of others I can use interchangeably with the colors I generally wear."

Outside, the storm still raged, a typical Northern California drencher that turned overfull storm drains into eddying whirlpools and intersections into hopeless gridlocks. But bundled into a raincoat, Paula was warm and dry when Amy let her out at the curb, and by the time they rendezvoused at the silk scarf counter, she was beginning to feel almost festive.

It was the first time, she realized, since Belinda's death nearly three weeks earlier, that she'd allowed herself to focus on anything so mindless as shopping, and she had to admit there was a certain comfort in the ordinariness of the task. By the time they had chosen a handful of colorful scarves, Amy, too, was having a good time, and they browsed happily through the lingerie department and into costume jewelry and cosmetics.

Before they realized it, it was three o'clock, and they looked at each other like guilty schoolgirls. Amy made a dash for the car as Paula waited just inside the door.

It was bad enough she'd missed the early run-through for the six o'clock broadcast; Nally was probably running around frantically, wondering where she was. On top of it, she'd agreed to see Mike Shaffer sometime between two and four, and he was probably standing around in the corridors cooling his heels and getting in everybody's way.

She should have telephoned, she realized with a pang, looking back into the store. But by that time, Amy had pulled up to the curb, and it seemed to make more sense to just keep going.

Amy Takehara was a good driver, but traffic was hideously snarled and what should have been a ten-minute trip stretched into nearly half an hour. Paula was surprised at her own agility getting out of the car. It was amazing, she thought, as she got into the elevator, what a healthy little dose of frustration could do for the human spirit.

She had hoped she might be able to sort of sidle into the studio without a lot of fanfare, find Nally, apologize for her tardiness, and get on about her business. But she sensed something unusual in the atmosphere the moment she stepped into the corridor: a mix of hushed activity and forced energy that set off alarm bells in her head.

She didn't see Nally, but Betty Lou, who would normally be scurrying around at this time of day, was slumped over the reception desk, her red hair splayed over her arms. When Paula tapped her on the shoulder the girl seemed to look up reluctantly.

Paula frowned, growing even more alarmed at the sight of Betty Lou's tear-streaked face. "What—"

"Deirdre," she managed. "I can't believe it" *Betty Lou blinked and burst into tears.*

It was minutes before Paula could piece it together; the boy who fell into the reservoir, Nally's decision to send Izzy and Deirdre, the wind, the rain, Deirdre's fall.

"She was dead before she got to the bottom," Izzy told Paula tonelessly. The veteran cameraman shook his head. "I tried—but there was nothing I could do!" He ran a hand over his deeply creased face. "She must have slipped on those damn wet rocks. By the time I saw her falling, it was too late. There wasn't a damn thing I could do. . . ."

Around them, the KSFO staff moved with grim deliberateness. It was already after four. Despite the shock, there was the six o'clock show to do, and the usual complement of sound and light checks, makeup, costumes, and script updates.

Paula picked up a script from Betty Lou and headed down the corridor to her dressing room, where she tossed the sheaf of papers on a low table and sat heavily in a chair.

It was the kind of thing that happened once in a while, a freak, unforeseeable accident—the same kind of accident that sent that unsuspecting twelve-year-old into the roiling, storm-swollen waters. But Deirdre, for all her youth and exuberance, knew better than to take chances, and Paula, while she was still stunned over the loss of her colleague, was also vaguely uneasy.

There were two pink message slips near the telephone on the table. Idly, she picked them up.

The first was from Zach. Stu Snyder had put an offer on the table. *"Call soonest to review terms and talk about a counter."*

She stared at the slip of paper, which weeks ago would have made her dizzy with happiness, but which she now viewed with detached calm as just one more thing to contend with.

The second message was from Mike Shaffer. God, she'd forgotten all about him! Sorry, he'd been caught at a road closure in the storm and had decided to return home. Would she please call at her earliest convenience and set another time for them to meet?

Amy came in, her umbrella dripping, looking unusually subdued. She must have heard the news, and though she'd only just met Deirdre, she was clearly affected by the tragedy. "How awful," she murmured. "Are you okay, Paula? Would you like a cup of coffee or something?"

Paula shook her head and stood up unsteadily. She needed to get ready for makeup. She needed to stop thinking about Synder and Mike and Belinda and Ted and Lissa. She even, she thought, as she slipped out of her dress, had to stop thinking about what had happened to Deirdre.

It was then that she realized what had been nagging at her and making her so uneasy. She sat like a stone and put her hands to her head to try to stop the roaring in her ears.

Yesterday, in this very room, she had given Deirdre a phone number. Paula felt the room begin to spin. Now Deirdre was dead.

Somehow Paula delivered the six o'clock script, with its double-barreled message of gloom; escalating fear for the boy in those rushing waters who had not yet been found and mourning for the reporter who had plunged to her death while attempting to cover the story.

It was all she could do not to choke on the words. Had Deirdre merely *plunged* to her death? Or had she been helped by an unseen hand because she'd been poking around where someone didn't want her looking?

She cornered Izzy. Was he absolutely certain he had seen no one else when Deirdre fell? No stranger—no hand, no arm reaching out as if to keep her from falling?

Izzy shook his mane of gray hair. No one. He had seen no one. He'd been stowing away his gear when he heard a muffled sound. When he looked up, Deirdre was tumbling down.

She called friends at channels two and six. Had they covered the reservoir story? Yes, they thought they remembered seeing Deirdre, but hadn't noticed anything unusual. They were so sorry, what an awful thing, what a horrible, freakish accident. . . .

At seven, from somewhere, Sam appeared, rain dripping off his raincoat collar and glistening in his hair. He held her for a moment, kissed her gently, and murmured words of understanding in her ear.

No, she didn't want to go out to dinner. She

couldn't eat a bite. It was probably silly, but she was half afraid she was to blame for Deirdre's death.

He listened to her, held her some more, sat with her in her dressing room. When she was feeling better, he called for Amy and sent her downstairs for sandwiches.

"I have to get back to my office in Seaview." His fingers grazed Paula's cheeks. "But I promised you a full investigation into all this, and there's already progress, I promise you."

He wrote his Seaview address and phone number on the back of a Tartan business card. It seemed strange to Paula, as she toyed with the card, to realize she didn't know where he lived.

"I expect to have a full report by the weekend," he told her. "Call me the minute you get there."

She took the call from Mike Shaffer a little before eight o'clock.

"I just heard the news, Paula. I'm very sorry. It's really a nasty storm. But I'd like to try again tomorrow, if you think you can spare me some time."

She thought a minute. Mike had his own agenda. His only thought was for his client. Still, if he'd learned anything that might help her. . . . "Fine. Tomorrow will be fine."

It was pouring, a driving, drenching downpour . . . She was standing at the bottom of a hill . . . Thunder rumbled overhead, then exploded in a deafening crescendo. In the next instant, she could see Lissa illuminated in a flash of lightning.

Lissa was standing at the crest of the hill, dressed in a thin, little pinafore, her chubby arms reaching out, her hair whipping about her face . . . She

seemed to be crying . . . Piteous wails floated
away on the wind . . .

  Pauullaaa!

  Paula sat up in bed, breathing hard, and found
herself staring into the darkness.

CHAPTER

~28~

By morning the storm had given way to a feeble, early spring. Fleecy clouds clung tenaciously to the deep green hills across the bay, but the city, scrubbed and fresh-faced, was washed in hopeful sunlight.

Paula stood at her bedroom window. A wren picked its way across her lawn. Across the street a little boy was taking a headstrong beagle puppy for a walk.

Just after dusk the night before, the boy in the reservoir had been found, miraculously clinging to a mid-sized boulder in the north fork of the reservoir more than four hours and seven miles from where he had fallen in.

He was said to be in shock and the extent of his injuries had yet to be determined, but while the KSFO crew was still reeling from what had happened to Deirdre, the story of the boy's successful rescue had lent a note of optimism to the ten o'clock broadcast.

It had cheered Paula, too, but not enough to allow her to rest easily. She shivered, recalling with startling clarity the nightmare that had wakened her: Lissa, buffeted by the wind and the rain, crying and calling her name. The time had come. Decisions must be made. She could not put them off any longer.

She glanced at her bedside clock. It was not yet eight o'clock, but she'd made one decision already. She was going home to Seaview, to confront Ted Raymond once and for all and to find out, with or without help from Sam Pierce and Mike Shaffer, what had happened to Belinda and why.

Amy knocked and opened the bedroom door. "Do you need anything before I get dressed?"

Paula shook her head. "No, you go ahead. And throw a few things into a bag. We're going up to Seaview for a day or two. There are some things I have to do."

She called Zach at home. "Yes, I got your message about Stu Snyder, but I can't think about it yet. . . . I know, I appreciate everything you're doing, but I have to get my life back together. Do me a favor, Zach, and call Nally. I'm going to have to miss today's broadcasts. I'm going up to Seaview. There are some things I have to do. I hope to be back tomorrow. I'll call you."

She called Mike Shaffer and told him not to bother to come into San Francisco. She was going to Seaview and would contact him. She wrote down the addresses and phone numbers he gave her so she could reach him at his office or at home.

Finally she called Ted. He told her he was just leaving to drop Lissa at preschool and go to work.

"I need to see you, Ted. We need to talk."

He sounded strained. "I have a really busy day."

But Paula insisted and at last he agreed to meet her at home at noon. Judy Morrissey would be picking Lissa up, but he wouldn't have much time . . .

In an hour she and Amy were on the road. They would be in Seaview in plenty of time to pick up her Honda from the auto body shop, then make arrangements to return the rental car and be at Ted's house in time.

Paula leaned back into the bucket seat. She had made a promise to Sam. Now she was breaking it, but she refused to believe she was putting herself in any danger.

Even if Ted had murdered Belinda, he would certainly have more sense than to accost Paula in his house.

And if it wasn't Ted? What if Ted was a pawn in a game masterminded by Davidson? Was Deirdre's death a less than subtle warning that he could get to Paula at any time?

She shuddered, only dimly aware of the landscape rushing past her. And then there was Lissa. Dear God, what was she to do about Lissa?

The voice on the phone was purely panicked. It first angered and then annoyed him.

"She's coming here. Paula. She wants to talk. She'll be at my house at noon."

"Then you'll tell her what you know, just as we discussed it. Nothing more, nothing less."

"But it's falling apart. That public defender. He's been asking a lot of questions. We have to talk—"

"All right. We'll talk. But get yourself together. I

told you from the beginning, you can count on me. Relax. I'll be in touch."

He hung up the phone. Ted was right. It was, indeed, falling apart. But there was plenty of time. He picked up the phone and dialed a number in Sausalito.

There was a sheaf of paperwork waiting at the auto body shop but Paula did her best to hurry through it. She had not seen her car since the accident, but she knew it had to have been a mess, and she was grateful to see it looking just as it had when she'd gotten into it that rainy evening.

But there was little time to think about it. She made arrangements for the rental agency to pick up their car at the body shop. Then they moved their bags from the rental to the Honda and climbed into the front seat. It was a quarter of twelve when Amy drew up to the curb in front of the Raymond house.

"Do you want me to come in?" Amy set the brake.

Paula deliberated. No matter what came of it, she needed to talk to Ted alone. But afterward, she realized, there was a good possibility she might no longer be welcome in his house. "No," she told Amy. "Take the car and go do some local sight-seeing. I shouldn't be more than an hour or two. Come back for me between one and two."

Amy tossed her the keys. "Nothing doing. Enough driving for one morning. The storm is over, the weather is lovely, and I could use the walk."

"It's up to you." Paula shrugged, giving her some general directions. "If you get tired, you can take a bus back—the number three from downtown. Get off at the intersection of Clark and Rutledge, right there across the street."

She watched Amy set off down the street. Ted's car was not in the driveway. Dreading that nothing would ever be the same, Paula dug in her purse for the key.

CHAPTER

—29—

There were dark circles under Ted's eyes and an odd pallor to his skin, a gray-white pastiness Paula had never seen in all the years she had known him—not even when she'd found him looking so strained on the night of Belinda's death.

For a moment she was alarmed. "Ted, are you all right?"

He nodded, pacing around the small living room, his gaze everywhere but on her. "I'm fine. . . . Okay, Paula, why are you here? Let's get this out in the open. I'm tired of pussyfooting around you, knowing you hate my guts."

Paula moved forward on the sofa. "Ted, please, I don't hate you—"

"Oh, yes, Paula, yes, you do. You'd like to kick my teeth in. You're just like Belinda—you think I'm the scum of the earth because I took money to stall that refinery inspection."

Stunned, Paula could feel her jaw drop.

"Yes, all right, I took money. Fifty-thousand bucks.

It was stupid, I admit it. I admitted it to Belinda. I don't even know now *why* I did it, except that—except it was so easy."

"But Lissa goes to school right near there!" Paula shrilled. "Hundreds of children do—less than a mile from that god-awful mess, that cesspool of contamination!"

Ted pleaded with her, his voice begging. "Paula, I didn't know it. I didn't realize how bad it was until all the testing was done, and by then it was too late. Do you think I would have exposed Lissa—or *anybody's* kids—if I had known the site was so poisoned?"

Paula could feel her thoughts tumbling forward, tumbling the way Deirdre had tumbled . . . the way she herself had tumbled into a ditch the night her car sailed off the highway.

"What did Belinda say?" she demanded. "What did she say when you told her?"

"She was frantic—"

"Did she threaten to expose you, Ted? To leave you? To put you *both* behind bars?" Paula rose unsteadily to her feet, and shouted over the roaring in her ears. *"Which one of you killed her, Ted? You or Wynn Davidson?"*

Ted's face, drained of color, took on an inhuman cast. "No, Paula, you've got it wrong. Danny Gentry killed her! That slimy, perverted half-wit killed her! He stabbed her to death in that kitchen!"

But Paula knew better. It was not Danny Gentry who had torn her mailbox apart. It was not Danny Gentry who had forced her off the road, and perhaps helped Deirdre to her death.

"No, Ted." She looked at him with loathing. "You did it. You and your friends. And as God is my witness, before I'm through I'll know who held the knife. . . ."

Time and space seemed to hold very still. He stared at her for a long moment. Then he turned on his heel, moved to the door, and slammed it thunderously behind him.

She sank down heavily, breathing hard, her arm beginning to throb as if the pain of what she had just discovered was seeping into her bones. The Ted Raymond she had once known had turned into a madman. There was no way she could stay, and Lissa—dear God! There was no way she could leave Lissa with him.

Ted would fight her. He would never allow her to take Lissa quietly. But there had to be a way, because she couldn't leave her with a madman—or worse, a murderer.

A lawyer could advise her . . . a lawyer. Mike Shaffer! Mike Shaffer was a lawyer! With her good hand, she pawed through her purse until she found the numbers he'd given her.

She dialed his office first. Yes, he was in. He answered his phone on the second ring.

"Mike, this is Paula Carroll. I'm here at the Raymond house, and I need to talk to you, but I'm not—I'm not sure I can drive."

He didn't hesitate. "Don't even try. I'll be there in less than ten minutes."

She looked at her watch. Ten minutes after one. Amy could be back at any time. But if Ted came back and found her here with Mike, he might fly into another rage.

No, she and Mike would have to get out of there, if only for a little while. She would ask Mike to leave a note on the windshield of her car instructing Amy, once she got back, to wait here until she returned.

And she *would* return. She would have to come back. She would be coming back for Lissa. There was no way she was leaving Seaview without Lissa in her arms.

Lissa would be out of preschool by now. She should be at Judy Morrissey's. To reassure herself that Lissa was all right, Paula decided to call. But where was the number? She didn't have it. Where was the telephone directory? And then she remembered Belinda's address book, the one Judy'd retrieved from the thrift shop.

Moving as quickly as she could manage, Paula plucked the little book from its shelf; Manoff, Mayfield, Morrissey, yes! She tossed the book onto the counter and dialed from the kitchen phone.

There was no answer, but a message came on after the third ring. "Judy, this is Paula." She spoke evenly. "I'll be at the Raymond house by three o'clock. Please have Lissa home by then. I'm taking her to San Francisco."

She had scrawled the note for Amy and was waiting at the curb when Mike drove up. Watching him place the note under her windshield wiper, she got into his car.

He drove up Rutledge for several miles to the canyon road Paula remembered, an old ribbon of highway overhung with trees that wound its way steeply to the canyon's crest.

In a woodsy glen thick with pines very near the top, he turned sharply to the left onto a dirt road that led to a small clearing.

She must have looked baffled. In their high school days, kids used to come up here to neck.

He looked at her and laughed. "My humble abode," he said, setting the brake. "It's not fancy, but it's quiet and private and I get the feeling that's what you had in mind."

She let herself be led through a small, neatly furnished cabin onto a large wooden deck that overlooked the arroyo.

At another time she would have been charmed by the sheer and breathtaking beauty of it, but now she sank into a redwood deck chair. Mike disappeared inside for a moment and came back with a couple of cans of soda.

Paula shook her head, then looked straight at Mike. "Danny Gentry did not kill Belinda," she said without preamble. "It was Ted or Wynn Davidson, I'm still not sure which, though I think they may have planned it together."

"I knew it wasn't Danny." He put the sodas on a wooden table. "Why don't you tell me what you know."

Paula sighed. "There isn't time. Mike, I'm asking you to trust me. Sam Pierce has people looking into it, and I promise I'll tell you everything we find out. When the time comes, if you think it will help, I'll even tell it in court." She looked at him earnestly. "But right now I need advice. It's very, very important."

He sat down facing her. "What can I do?"

"I want to take Lissa to San Francisco. I can't leave her here with Ted. I think—I'm afraid it may not be safe. But I need to know my legal rights."

Mike cocked his head. "Your legal rights? You have none. Ted is her father."

Paula swallowed. "No. He isn't. And he hates—he's furious with her mother."

Mike was looking at her, clearly puzzled. God, where was she to begin? Blinking against the string of tears, she gazed down into the arroyo. . . .

She remembered the day before their college graduation. She had called Belinda at the small apartment off campus she had rented right after her wedding.

"Hey, Mrs. Raymond." She'd kept her tone light. *"Still feel like a brand-new bride?"*

"Hi, Paula!" There was a smile in Belinda's voice. *"Mrs. Raymond! I'm still getting used to it. Doesn't it have a lovely sound?"*

"It does. . . . Look, Belinda, there's something I need to talk to you about."

Belinda hadn't hesitated. *"Come on over."*

It had been the longest three-block walk Paula had ever taken, less because she regretted her condition than because the irony was so painful: There was Belinda, her best friend, afraid she'd never be able to get pregnant—and here was Paula, on the brink of a career, who was going to have a baby.

But Belinda, as usual, had taken it in stride. *"It's Anton's baby, isn't it?"*

Paula had nodded, with little regret for the spoiled ambassador's son who had loved her passionately until he found out she was pregnant and then gone off to join his father in Algeria.

"What are you going to do?"

Paula had shrugged. *"I haven't made up my mind."*

"Well, I have an idea." Belinda was flushed with excitement. *"I have the most wonderful idea."*

And in the end, it *had* seemed perfect, even Ted agreed, for Paula to have the child and get on with her career while Mr. and Mrs. Raymond took "their" baby with them when Belinda joined him in San Diego.

If Mike had an opinion, he did not show it. "I've never regretted it," she told him. "Lissa has always been a very happy child, and Belinda was a wonderful mother. . . ."

She didn't tell Mike how many nights she had lain awake in her bed, aching for the child who was bringing so much happiness into Belinda's life. She didn't tell him how hard she had worked to force herself to take a backseat until, slowly, the reality of the situation had simply become a fact of life.

Whatever Mike thought, he kept it to himself. "Did Belinda and Ted adopt Lissa?"

"Yes, but—"

He shook his head. "Then legally you have no claim—even if you are her natural mother."

Paula was horrified. "But that's not right! She could be living with a murderer."

"He hasn't been charged."

"But she could be in danger."

"Has he ever hurt her?"

"Well, no—"

He held up a hand. "There isn't a judge who'd let you take her under those circumstances. Not without reasonable proof that Ted's committed a crime or that there's reason to believe he might harm her."

Paula reflected. "He took a bribe. He admitted that much to me. And his delay in inspecting the refinery site put Lissa—and others—in jeopardy."

Mike drummed his fingers on the table. His brown eyes radiated sympathy. "I don't think that's enough at this point, Paula. I'll research it if you want. But it seems to me that unless or until Ted is charged with a crime, there's just not much you can do."

Paula listened to the call of the birds. The sound seemed to echo from the canyon. "I see," she said finally, getting up from her chair. "Well, thank you for your time."

"Paula—"

She was already moving through the cabin. "May I ask you to drive me back? Amy will be waiting, and maybe Lissa . . ." She let her voice trail off.

They were mostly silent driving back to Ted's house.

"Look, Paula—" Mike began.

Paula cut him off. "It's all right, Mike. I have some other ideas."

It occurred to her that she had not called Sam to let him know she was in town. Sam would have news for her. He'd promised he would, and he was the kind of man who got things done. He was bound to have turned up something that would help, some indisputable proof.

Her heart leaped at the sight of the patrol car parked in front of Ted's house. Lissa! Something had happened to Lissa! She scrambled out of Mike's car.

The officers who approached her were both cut from the same cloth, clean-cut, blond, and impassive. "Mrs. Raymond?" The taller one began. "Are you Mrs. Belinda Raymond?"

Paula stared. She wanted to speak, but the words wouldn't come.

Mike stepped forward. "Excuse me, Officer. Mrs. Raymond is deceased. My name is Mike Shaffer, and this is Paula Carroll. She's . . . a very close friend of the family."

The officer fidgeted.

"Is there something wrong?"

The officer looked confused. Finally his gaze settled on Paula. "Ma'am—I'm afraid there's been an accident."

CHAPTER

~ 30 ~

Paula had wanted to shake Ted until his teeth rattled. She had wanted to see him behind bars. She had wanted him as far away from Lissa as he could get, but she had never wished him dead, and the news that he *was* dead hit her with such force that it literally left her reeling.

From somewhere, arms reached out to steady her. She managed to find her key and the next thing she knew she was on the cream-colored sofa in what had once been Belinda's living room.

Ted had been driving on the coast highway south of town, too fast, as far as the officers could tell. He may have misjudged a turn, or maybe he'd simply lost control, but he'd barreled off the edge of a cliff.

Barreled off the edge of a cliff. Paula closed her eyes. *Another accident. And Ted was gone.* She felt her head begin to spin.

"Are you all right, ma'am?" The officers were watching her. "Is there anything else we can do?

Anyone else we should call, perhaps—a relative of Mr. Raymond's?"

Paula shook her head. She thought she remembered that Ted had had a brother, but the two had not been close and to Paula's knowledge there was little if any contact between them. "I don't think so," she said. "I don't think there's anyone. Just—his daughter. And me."

"His daughter, ma'am?"

Mike broke in. "Officer, Mr. Raymond's daughter is only four years old. She recently lost her mother and, frankly, I think it would be a lot more damaging for her to find you here in her living room than to learn about this . . . tragedy from Ms. Carroll, whom she knows and trusts."

The officers nearly fell all over themselves in their haste to get out of the house. If the situation were not so grave, Paula might have thought it was funny.

As it was, she turned to Mike and drew in a shaky breath. "Well," she managed. "This changes a number of things. Including Lissa's situation. I don't imagine there will be too much resistance to my taking her home with me now."

"Paula—" Mike began.

But Paula cut him off. "Please. One problem at a time."

He nodded. "Okay. Did the Raymonds have wills?"

"I believe they did, yes. They named me Lissa's godmother, and they made it clear they intended for me to act as her guardian in the event—in the event of their deaths."

She looked at her watch. "Lissa will be here soon. I left a message with the neighbor who's babysitting to have her home at three."

Mike's voice was soft. "Would you like me to stay?

I think—Lissa sort of liked me. At least I thought she did, that day at the ice cream store. . . ." His voice trailed off.

Paula swallowed over a lump in her throat. "Yes. I think she did. Thank you, Mike. I appreciate the offer, but I'd rather—I'd rather talk to her alone."

In the end, he offered to go down to the courthouse and talk to a juvenile court judge. Until the will turned up, he would ask that Paula be granted temporary custody.

When he'd gone, two things occurred to Paula. One was that Amy was late. The other was that she needed to call Sam. He would want to know what had happened.

Refusing to think about what Ted's death meant, she dug around in her purse. But she couldn't seem to find the card Sam had given her in her dressing room the day before. Frowning, she dumped the contents of her purse out onto the coffee table, but it wasn't there and she couldn't remember the name of his Seaview company.

Belinda's address book! She went to the kitchen and began to flip through the pages. *BELINDA AT WORK: TATTERSALL INDUSTRIES*. Paula dialed the number.

He was on the phone in seconds. "Paula, where are you?"

"I'm in Seaview. At Ted's house. . . ."

"Then you know—"

"Yes."

"It's all over the local news. I've been frantic trying to reach you."

"Lissa," she murmured. "I expect her any minute. I don't know what we'll do after I tell her."

"Do nothing," he told her. "Wait for me. I can be there in twenty minutes."

She felt better when she'd hung up. It would be good to have Sam here. Apart from Paula, he was as near to family as anyone Lissa had ever had—and Paula had to admit she was going to be glad to be with someone she could lean on.

Idly, she turned the pages of Belinda's little address book, smiling at the familiar handwriting.

Under the *D*s, she found the address and phone number for Duncan Associates in Las Vegas—and an arrow drawn to the facing page, where Belinda had jotted a note in the margin.

Holding it closer, Paula squinted to read the lightly penciled note. *SCOTS*, it looked like. . . . *HLND, how strg! P ck out DCN, HLND, MAC.* . . .

"Paula!"

Lissa sounded so gleeful that Paula's heart plunged to her shoes. God, this child had already been through so much. How could she stand any more?

Judy's eyes were wide and worried. Apparently, she'd already heard the news. Paula reached out and gave her a hug. Then she bent down, smoothed Lissa's hair and folded her into her arms.

Reluctantly, highway patrolman Hank Chandler took the sheaf of papers. If there was one thing he hated to do, it was clean up somebody else's mess.

Apparently some poor dude had gone off a cliff somewhere on the coast highway, and the responding officers were making a house call to let his wife know she was a widow. Grumbling, Chandler took the reports to get them entered into the log. He was halfway through the first page when he began to pay serious attention.

From skidmarks at the scene, the officers believed the victim had been traveling at high speed; so much so that when his vehicle hit bottom, there wasn't too much left of it to inspect. But a witness near the scene had thought another vehicle might have been involved. He told the officers he thought *a big Cadillac with dark, tinted windows* had been riding the victim's tail—so closely, he said, that he'd shaken his head at the irresponsible way some people drive.

The words seemed to leap off the page. *A big Cadillac with dark, tinted windows.* He scanned the report for more information, and he found it at the top of page two. When pressed, the witness thought the license plate on the Caddy might have read, DADDY or LADDY.

It was information the responding officers would routinely check out, Chandler knew, running the plate number through the Department of Motor Vehicles to find the registered owner. But Chandler wasn't about to wait for them. This was one mess he wouldn't mind cleaning up.

CHAPTER

⟵31⟶

Ordinarily Paula would not have taken the call—not this afternoon, anyway. She was still reeling from the impact of Ted's death and reluctant to interpret what it meant.

Lissa listened, dry-eyed, when Paula explained what had happened: that her daddy had gone to be with Belinda, but that Paula was here to take care of her.

Without a word, Lissa had looked for her Pooh Bear and dragged him over to the sofa, where she'd climbed up, closed her eyes, and promptly fallen asleep.

Baffled, Paula watched her daughter sleep, supposing the odd reaction was Lissa's way of cushioning the pain, of distancing herself, at least for a while, until she was able to deal with it.

Paula knew she was going to have to call Dr. Irvin, the psychologist Lissa liked so well. She'd been wanting to do that anyway, and now there was no choice. She was the only parent Lissa had left, and she was going to need all the help she could get to help her daughter through this.

She looked at her watch. Sam would be here soon. And where in the world was Amy? In the short time she'd known her, Amy had proven to be the soul of reliability. It simply wasn't like her to be more than an hour late without so much as a phone call.

So when the phone did ring, Paula jumped and, fearful of waking Lissa, moved as quickly as she could to the kitchen.

She heard her own intake of breath when the caller identified himself. The name Hank Chandler meant nothing to her, but the words California Highway Patrol did, and Paula braced herself for the awful news that something had happened to Amy.

She blinked, confounded, as Chandler went on about the Caddy with dark, tinted windows, and eventually she realized the patrolman was not calling about either Ted or Amy. He was the CHP officer in charge of investigating Paula's own rainy-night accident.

"With every case, you gotta hope for a break," Chandler told her soberly. "And I think this time we mighta got it with a car somebody saw this afternoon."

He sounded disappointed when Paula told him the license plate LADDY meant nothing to her.

"Oh," he said. "Doesn't sound like the license plate of anybody you know?"

She told him it didn't.

"Well," he persisted. "What about Highlands, Inc.? That's the name of the company who's the registered owner of the car with this particular plate."

Paula shook her head. "No, I don't think so. I mean I don't recognize the names. . . ."

But in the next instant she felt an odd prickling creep up the back of her scalp. LADDY . . . Highland . . . *Scottish names*. She reached for Belinda's address book.

SCOTS, Belinda had penciled in the margin. *SCOTS* . . . Scottish names! HLD—Could that be Highland? And DCN—Duncan? Paula blinked. Had Belinda made a connection between the Scottish-sounding names? Between the companies?

She stared down at the cryptic jottings: *P ck out DCN, HLD, MAC.* . . . She could almost hear Belinda's voice, *"Paula check out Duncan—Highland—Mac,"* . . . and the meaning of it so overwhelmed her that she thought she was going to gag.

Gold lettering on a chic oak door. *Mac and Lady Mac, Superior Sportswear*: Macbeth and Lady Macbeth, characters in a Scottish castle . . . Tartan Companies, Tattersall Industries, names for Scottish plaids . . . and Highland and Duncan, links in a chain, all owned by the same man . . . a man she had alerted from the moment she'd started talking about Ted's involvement with Wynn Davidson.

No, she told herself. Not Sam. Not Sam, who said he cared for her! But every fiber of her knew it was true, and it took her breath away. Holding the back of a chair to steady herself, she managed to speak into the phone. "Call the Seaview Police. Tell them . . . Oh God—I don't know . . ."

Her mind raced. Sam was on his way. He would be here very soon. She had to get out of there, and she couldn't leave Lissa, and Amy was nowhere to be seen.

The car keys—yes! Her car keys were here! They were right there on the coffee table, just where she'd left them a while ago when she'd dumped out the contents of her purse!

Lissa was curled in a heap on the sofa, her arm curved protectively around Pooh. Yanking her own arm out of its sling, Paula managed to lift the sleeping child. Wincing, she carried her out to the curb and put her down on the backseat of her car.

Scrambling into the driver's seat, she locked the doors and turned the key in the ignition, gritting her teeth against the searing pain that shot up the length of her arm.

Her first thought was to get to the police station, and she pulled into the left lane, but as she prepared to make the turn, a car moved up suddenly from her left, blocking her way into the intersection.

She didn't know where the other car had come from, but she stepped hard on the accelerator, figuring she would make the left turn at the next available street.

But the same car drew up on her left, narrowly missing her bumper, and when she looked up into her rearview mirror, she recognized Sam in the driver's seat.

Sam, she acknowledged with a sinking heart, whose empire was far larger than Belinda knew; Sam, who had murdered Belinda in cold blood because she was so close to the truth.

Suddenly Paula knew, too, what the letter stolen from her mailbox had said. Belinda had sent her a letter—a letter she'd never received—and it had undoubtedly asked her to look into the corporate links between Duncan Associates and Sam's companies.

Paula wondered whether there ever *was* a Wynn Davidson or whether Sam himself had been the conduit, setting off a maelstrom of lies and violence that had claimed the lives of three people and played havoc with so many others.

Blinking back tears, Paula swerved to the right, flinching at the screech of tires. There was more than one way to skin a cat! She would turn right at every corner until she was headed toward town.

But Sam's Lincoln outmaneuvered her, and her arm hurt with every turn. Aware of Lissa in the backseat, she felt her panic rising.

What if I get off the road? she thought. *What if I just pull over? What is he going to do, pull out a gun, and shoot me in broad daylight?*

But before she could react, she was forced to veer sharply to avoid an oncoming car, and she found herself shooting across an intersection onto the canyon road.

She glanced back over her shoulder. Miraculously, Lissa was still asleep. Now she was in a secluded area, but she was headed toward Mike Shaffer's house. If she could somehow manage to outdistance Sam, maybe she would be all right. Maybe she would recognize the surprising left turn that led to Mike's property. Clamping her lips together, she pressed her foot to the floorboard and shot forward up the hill.

It had been a long time since Paula had prayed, but she found herself praying now. *Dear God, I gave my child away once. Don't let me lose her again. . . .*

Trees, brush, overhanging branches blended together in a blur as she rounded turn after hairpin turn, only to glance in her rearview mirror and see that Sam was still behind her.

This was how Ted had died, she realized with heart-wrenching certainty: rounding a curve on the coast highway with a car closing in on him—the way a big car with dark, tinted windows had forced her off the highway in the rain . . .

Screeching around a curve, her eyes searched the brush for an almost hidden clearing, the place where Mike had turned onto a dirt road as they neared the crest of the hill.

"Pauullaa! Where *are* we?" Lissa sounded frightened. "Why are we going so fast?" She was standing up in the backseat, obscuring Paula's view.

"Please, sweetheart, sit down," she begged. Frowning, she scanned the road ahead of her. Was that the turn, just up ahead? *Please,* she prayed, holding her breath, *let it be the right place!* If it wasn't, she knew, she could plunge into the arroyo, taking Lissa with her.

Tires screeching, she swerved left. Yes! Yes, it was a road! Slumping forward, she put her foot on the brake as she neared the driveway to the cabin, hoping she had enough distance between them for Sam to have missed the turn.

Lissa was wailing from the backseat. Paula turned around to reach for her. Her heart sank as Sam's Lincoln slowed to a stop behind her.

CHAPTER

~32~

There were two things Mike had concluded from his experience as a public defender:

First, there was a limit to the number of accidents that could reasonably be accepted as accidents.

Second, a guy who committed one crime was apt to commit another—if only to try to cover up the tracks he hadn't covered up the first time.

Mike thought about that as he stepped hurriedly down the cracked, stone steps of the courthouse, an order in his pocket granting Paula Carroll temporary custody of Lissa Raymond.

The weather had turned warm again after the rains. He felt the sun on his back through his jacket, and he wiped away the fine mist that was beading on his brow.

Take Ted Raymond's accidental death, for instance, so soon after his wife's murder. Add Paula's accident and the accidental death of a reporter Paula worked with, and it came to a few more accidents than Mike could readily swallow.

So he had to figure that whoever killed Belinda and tried to fob it off on Danny was clever enough to engineer the other things and make them *look* like accidents.

He crossed the street against the light, to the loud protest of several motorists. Somebody was out there making all the right moves. If it wasn't Ted Raymond—and it wasn't likely the guy had engineered his own death—then it was time that Mike, for Paula's sake as well as Danny's, began to look further afield.

Harvey Nattlinger had come up with zero when he ran a make on Wynn Davidson. The guy was apparently a reputable Nevada attorney who headed up the Duncan operation—and apart from culpability in the refinery mess, there was no dirt on Duncan either.

But what if Duncan was a front operation for a bigger, hungrier conglomerate? Who was the viable common denominator for Belinda and Paula and Ted—and, by extension, to Paula's dead colleague, the reporter, Deirdre Adams?

An answer rippled slowly to the surface, like a porpoise from the depths of a swimming pool. Mike continued past his office and turned left, toward the jail. He could be off-base, but it was worth a try. He wanted to talk to Danny Gentry.

Dickie Hetherington uncoiled himself from his chair and gave him a jaunty salute. "Yo, counselor. How's tricks? Anything new on your girlfriend?"

"My girlfriend."

"Paula! Word is she was talking to a CHP, and I guess she came a little unglued—told the Chippie to call the boys upstairs like she might be in some kind of trouble."

Mike frowned. "What are you talking about, Dickie? Where is Paula now?"

Dickie shrugged. "Damned if I know! You want me to call upstairs?"

The desk sergeant was no help. Paula Carroll had been at the Raymond house when she talked to the CHP. She wasn't there now. All units had been advised, but she hadn't been spotted yet.

Dickie shrugged his bony shoulders. "You want me to call the CHP?"

But Mike didn't wait. He headed out the door and sprinted across the street toward his car.

Lissa clambered over the front seat of the car and into Paula's arms. "Paula, you drived too fast," she scolded. "The p'liceman will give you a ticket!"

Paula wished a policeman *had*. "I'm sorry, sweetheart—" she began.

But Lissa was pointing a chubby finger. "And Sam! You drived too fast, too! What is this place, anyway? There are so many trees. Is this where you live, Sam?"

He had gotten out of his car, and he was ambling toward them like a man with all the time in the world. "No, honey, this is not where I live. But I know where we are. Don't you, Paula?"

Paula didn't respond. Pain shot through her elbow as she tried to draw Lissa closer. But when Sam reached out, Lissa wiggled away and jumped up into his arms.

Paula got up out of her car and flashed him a look of fury, but he didn't seem to notice. He was turning slowly, his gaze scanning the property.

"Look there," he said to Lissa, pointing toward the bottom of a slope. "Whoever lives here has some ducks! Why don't you run down to the pond and watch them while Paula and I talk?"

Lissa seemed to hesitate, but only for a second. Then she began to run. Paula wavered between fear for her safety and relief that Sam had let her go.

He seemed to read her mind. "Now, Paula, you know I would never hurt Lissa."

"Oh?" She thrust her chin up defiantly. "She could have been hurt in that chase!"

Sam chuckled. "That was fine driving, Paula, for a woman with only one good arm."

"Yes," she spat. "I had *two* good arms the last time you forced me off the road."

He smiled at her sadly. "You give me too much credit. I told you once, money opens doors. Unfortunately I can't take care of everything myself, but there are any number of people I can use."

The phrase infuriated her. "Like Ted?" she spat.

He shrugged. "Ted was weak. It took him awhile but he figured things out. Toward the end he was ready to fold."

"Not like Belinda."

"No," he agreed. "Belinda had the courage of her convictions. She wouldn't have cared that it could cost me forty million to clean up a little toxic waste—that a lifetime of building by a thrifty Scotsman could be gone in the blink of an eye."

"A lifetime of building—" Paula sputtered. "You killed her! You murdered Belinda."

He looked at Paula with infinite patience. "I had to. I had no choice. She would have done whatever it took to force me out in the open. As you would, Paula. You were two of a kind. I've always been drawn to strong women."

Paula turned away. Strong *dead* women. And weak, helpless men. . . .

She glanced around her, amazed to realize she was looking for somewhere to run. But there was only the woods and the chasm of the arroyo, and with a cast on, she couldn't outrun him. . . .

She shaded her eyes and looked toward the pond, where Lissa was sitting on her knees, clapping her hands as the little white ducks bobbed and dived beneath the surface. Paula drew a shuddering breath. The child had already endured so much. She prayed fervently she would never know it if she lost her mother twice. . . .

Sam was taking her by her good elbow, turning her in the opposite direction. "A little walk." He propelled her firmly. "A walk around the edge of the arroyo. A disabled woman . . . accidents happen . . . Lissa will understand. . . ."

Crazy schemes bumped around in her brain. A blow to his head with all her strength! Better yet, as he led her to the edge, she would duck and shove him out in front of her. . . .

She was mapping out the timing when they heard the sound, a low mechanical rumble. When she spun around, she saw a small sedan screech to a stop in the driveway—and behind it, the exquisitely flashing red lights of a black and white police car.

CHAPTER

33

"I love a woman with trim ankles." Mike carried a tray of salad fixings out to the deck and set it on the redwood table.

Paula had been watching a pair of wrens frolicking in a fir tree in the arroyo. She glanced down lazily at her bare left ankle, wrapped now with only the thinnest of bandages, and flexed her right hand into a tight fist just to prove to herself that she could. "Good thing you came along when you did that day," she smiled, "or I might have been contending with a lot worse than a couple of broken bones."

Mike handed her a head of lettuce, which she began tearing into a bowl. "No chance"—he shook his blond head—"I'm as dependable as the postman. It's a curse."

She watched him slice cucumber into neat, flat disks, fascinated by the way the sunlight glinted off the tiny, blond hairs around his knuckles. "Tell me again"—she went back to her chore—"how you figured out where I was."

He smiled. "Radar."

"Seriously," she said. "The police might never have found me on their own."

She had heard the story more than once, from Mike, from Harvey Nattlinger, even from Amy Takehara—how Mike had driven to the Raymond house and found Amy sitting on the curb, frantic, knowing that Paula would never have taken the car unless it had been an emergency.

"I figured you were trying to get away from somebody," Mike had told her, "and Sam Pierce was the only person I could think of who had a connection to all the principals—even to Danny, whom he easily maneuvered into going to Belinda's house with those balloons at precisely five o'clock on the day he killed her."

Paula looked off to her right, to the little pond at the bottom of the slope, where Lissa and Danny were feeding ducks. It would have been tragic if that gentle boy had actually had to stand trial.

"Incredible, isn't it?" Mike followed her line of sight. "Ted Raymond was Sam's ace in the hole—the most obvious suspect in Belinda's murder if the case against Danny fell apart. And when Ted began to fear he *was* going to be a suspect, Sam offered to *protect* him."

Paula nodded, still wondering at the ease with which Sam had engineered things. He had told Harvey Nattlinger that Ted was in his office during the time the murder was committed. Which was true, except that as it turned out, Ted was actually Sam's alibi. While Ted was cooling his heels in Sam's outer office, Sam had time to go to Belinda's house and kill her, knowing full well that Danny would be there in time for Ted to find him.

"The only thing that's tough to believe"—Mike dumped the cucumbers into the salad bowl—"was that Ted Raymond actually convinced himself that Danny had murdered Belinda."

"He wanted to believe it," Paula said. "Ted was weak. Sam knew that. He told me that himself. . . ."

Mike nodded. "And you, like Belinda and Deirdre before you, were getting too close to the truth. Sam's hired hand had blown his assignment the first time they decided to go after you. But when you got into your car *this* time, you gave Sam the chance to finish the job himself."

Paula knew that was true. "But I still don't understand how you knew I'd be up here at your place."

Mike shrugged. "I didn't know for sure, but you hadn't been spotted in town. I figured: (A) If *I* were Sam, and I wanted you alone, it wouldn't be in the city streets. And (B) If you were really making a bid to outrun him, you might have thought my place was a good bet."

"You did, eh?" Paula smiled seductively. She could have sworn Mike blushed.

But he met her gaze. "Well, I'm glad you'd been up here and sort of learned your way around that morning. And I'll tell you something else." He put a warm hand over hers. "I'm happy you're here now."

"Paula, Paula! Look what we found!" Lissa came running up to the deck and held up two perfect pinecones. "Can we take them home and show them to Amy? We can put them on the shelf over the fireplace!"

"Of course, sweetheart. Stay close to the house. Dinner will be ready soon."

Lissa pointed a chubby finger. "Danny found blueberries over there! Can we go pick some for dessert?"

Mike gave Paula a reassuring look. "Sounds like a great idea." He handed her a basket. "Pick as many as you can find. And Danny, you keep a close eye on her."

She skipped off in the direction of the pond, Danny close on her heels.

"How's it going with Danny?" Paula hefted a fat, red tomato Lissa had picked from Mike's garden that morning.

"Great. He's really terrific with plants. There's a chance the county will hire him. Till then, I'll be keeping him here with me. How about you—and Lissa?"

Paula nodded. "Lissa's doing fine. She seems to like her new school. And Amy's agreed to stay on for a while—for as long as we're in San Francisco."

Mike looked up from the carrot he was slicing. "As long as you're in San Francisco . . . I thought you'd just had an offer from a network?"

"I did. I turned it down. There's a new cable television station starting up here. They've offered me the job of executive producer, and it sounds like a wonderful challenge."

Mike smiled. "No kidding. Then you'll be moving back up here?"

She nodded, and his smile broadened. "Don't go away," he told her. "You wait right here while I go in and get us something to help us celebrate."

Paula leaned back into the canvas deck chair and gazed out across the arroyo, where the afternoon sun sent out kaleidoscopes of light as it filtered through the pines.

For the first time, she felt a bond with this place,

the place where she had grown up and where, it seemed, against impossible odds, she would be raising her own daughter.

One day soon, as Dr. Irvin had pointed out, she would have to find the words to tell Lissa, to help her understand the events that had blessed her with three parents and taken two of them away. For now, Paula was trying to accept it herself and to put the pain behind her.

Sam Pierce had been bound over for trial. He had hired a high-powered attorney. But despite his offer to liquidate assets to speed the refinery site cleanup, bail had been denied and with the number of witnesses the prosecution had lined up, it was doubtful he would ever be free again.

In the distance she could hear the song of the birds and Lissa's high-pitched chatter. They were good sounds, and she was alive to hear them. They filled her with a sense of well-being.

"Here we are!" Mike reached over and handed her a cold can of beer. He popped another can open, touched it to hers, and lifted it jauntily to his lips.

Paula looked at the basket of pretzels he'd placed on the redwood table. She began to laugh.

"What's funny?" he asked.

She was laughing too hard to answer. She could hear Belinda, as plain as day, just as if she were there with her: *"Listen, Paula, there's nothing wrong with champagne and caviar now and then. But there's a lot to be said for beer and pretzels on a warm spring afternoon!"*